"Go right on in, Lisa," said the Dean's secretary when I arrived at the gateway to Deandom.

I walked innocently into Saltonstall's opulently appointed inner sanctum. Instantly, my world turned upside down. I hardly noticed the thick Oriental carpet and the mahogany antique furniture. My attention was riveted on the woman sitting next to the Dean on his VIP couch.

She was dressed to kill in a nifty little black suit with a maroon silk blouse and gold dangly earrings. She sported dark hair, twisted in a low, stylish bun, a beaky nose, and a triumphant expression on her narrow face. It was Valerie Albrecht, my former boss and personal nemesis.

"Hello, David. What did you want to see me about?" I thought I knew what he was about to say, and the very idea made my stomach sink past my shoes into the floor.

He said it. "Lisa—Dr. Donahue—I wanted you to be the first to meet your new Director, Dr. Valerie Albrecht."

Director? Valerie? But I'd just filed my own application for the job! Suddenly I saw flashing lights at the corners of my eyes—clear signs that the migraine I'd been trying to avoid was about to snatch my brain and shred all rational thought.

"Lisa?" asked the Dean, clearly puzzled.

I snapped to attention and stuck out my hand. "Dr. Albrecht," I croaked," Welcome to Boston."

Val hazel eyes shone with amusement as she gripped my hand with painted talons. "Ms. Donahue," she responded silkily, refusing to acknowledge our identical academic titles. "I'm sure we'll make a fine team."

Wings

THE FALL OF AUGUSTUS

by

Sarah Wisseman

A Wings ePress, Inc.

Mystery novel

Wings ePress, Inc.

Edited by: Joan C. Afman
Copy Edited by: Leslie Hodges
Senior Editor: Leslie Hodges
Managing Editor: Karen Babcock
Executive Editor: Marilyn Kapp
Cover Artist: Jinger Heston

All rights reserved

Names, characters and incidents depicted in this book are products of the author's imagination or are used fictitiously. Any resemblance to actual events, locales, organizations, or persons, living or dead, is entirely coincidental and beyond the intent of the author or the publisher.

No part of this book may be reproduced or transmitted in any form or by any means, electronic or mechanical, including photocopying, recording, or by any information storage and retrieval system, without permission in writing from the publisher.

Wings ePress Books
http://www.wings-press.com

Copyright © 2009 by Sarah Wisseman
ISBN: 978-1-59705-615-1

Published In the United States Of America

October 2009

Wings ePress Inc.
403 Wallace Court
Richmond, KY 40475

Dedication

For the moms in my life: Carley, Janet, Jane, and Joy.

Acknowledgments

Once again, I thank my family and friends for putting up with me during the writing of this novel. Huge thanks to my writing partner, Molly MacRae, who critiqued each chapter as it evolved, and to Barbara D'Amato for reading the final manuscript. Their input improved the book enormously.

I also thank Shirley Jensen, Ottilia Schershel, and JoAnn Temple-Dennett, members of my online Sisters in Crime critique group, for numerous helpful comments and corrections. And last but never least, I thank all my museum colleagues who have shared so much over the years.

For the ongoing saga of Lisa and James, visit my website at www.sarahwisseman.com

One

Monday, January 13

The Emperor Augustus hovered over the elevator shaft. Light danced on his snow-white limbs and gaudy parade armor, and he hardly noticed the bonds that held him standing erect in an unusually shaped chariot.

"Ready?" I called to Dylan Luneau, who was poised at the top of the elevator shaft on the fourth floor.

"Almost!" said Dylan.

I heard a metallic clank as he adjusted the cables. Despite the frigid temperatures outside, I was sweating. And it wasn't because I'd just raced down the stairs from the fourth to the first floor of our ancient classroom building at Boston University.

Ellen Perkins—our conservator and my best buddy—stood next to me at the bottom of the shaft. Ellen's job was to make sure the elevator doors didn't close at the wrong time. She pushed one hand through her short blonde hair and held the other hand over the "open door" button. We both looked up apprehensively.

The enormous bulk of our biggest, heaviest plaster cast lurked overhead, invisible to us since the bottom of the open-sided platform filled our sky. Dylan, our museum's preparator and Ellen's current boyfriend, was in charge of moving the statue. I had to admit, he was pretty good with purely mechanical stuff. He'd successfully moved the Apollo Belvedere, festooned with deposits of pigeon shit (a result of being housed in a fourth floor attic museum with broken windows); that one had been easy because the Apollo could be broken down into sections. Moving the Primaporta Augustus, with its fancy drapery and outstretched arm—was much more dangerous.

"Who thought of this harebrained scheme, anyway?" I asked Ellen, just to make conversation.

"Lisa Donahue, how could you forget? It was Victor. He wouldn't agree to my suggestion of lifting the statues out with a crane through a hole in the roof. Too expensive." Ellen made a face.

Oh, yes. Victor Fitzgerald, our penny-pinching director, had finally agreed to remove the walls of the elevator car—a model almost as old as some of our artifacts—after careful measurements had convinced him that our biggest statues couldn't fit in the shaft any other way. Taking them down four flights of stairs in Wigglesworth Hall was out of the question; it would require a small army of expensive musclemen from Operations and Maintenance. Our puny university museum budget didn't allow for that kind of expenditure.

George Skirvin's whiny voice sounded from the top of the shaft. "Hey, Dylan, shouldn't there be a little more padding around the base of the statue?" George, a pudgy, sullen undergraduate student, acted as Dylan's assistant.

"Nah, it's okay, I've got it under control."

Of course Dylan *would* say that. He had an inflated sense of his abilities sometimes.

"You run down to the third floor so you can monitor the statue as we lower it," Dylan yelled to George.

This was our safeguard—to lower each statue floor-by-floor, checking its position at every level (except the second floor, which had no access to the elevator). The statue itself was balanced on a platform—the floor of the original elevator car—between Ethafoam bumpers to shield the plaster during its journey.

"Ready at the top!" called Dylan.

I pictured him in the fourth floor hallway, with other statue casts—the Laocoon, the Venus di Milo, and the Pieta—lurking in line behind him. The Laocoon was my personal favorite—it showed a Trojan priest and his two sons being strangled by sinister sea serpents. The priest was the poor guy who tried to warn Trojans not to bring the Greeks' gift of a giant wooden horse into their city; the serpents were sent by the god Poseidon, who was on the side of the Greeks.

Creaks from the cables mixed with murmurs from the other staff who were all on different floors. The acoustics of an open elevator shaft were peculiar, to say the least.

"Okay here!" replied George, from the third floor. He was a surprisingly fast runner despite his bulk.

"Ready at the bottom!" I replied, glancing behind me at the packing crate that stood ready to receive Augustus after he had descended the narrow shaft. Thank goodness the news media hadn't picked up on this event.

Uh-oh. Around the corner appeared my boss, Victor Fitzgerald, with Dean Saltonstall and two reporters bearing camcorders and notebooks.

"Don't look now," I whispered to Ellen.

She stuck her head out of the elevator. "Good grief!" she hissed. "Why can't they wait until the grand opening of the new museum?"

"They're probably hard-up for human interest stories," I said. "After all, no one has ever moved a whole pantheon of Greek gods and Roman emperors this way."

Susie Blake, our assistant director, waltzed up. She was as sleek as ever in a navy-blue pantsuit and matching suede pumps. Smoothing her salon-enhanced red curls, she chirped, "Now, now, Lisa. You know that publicity is always good for a university museum!'

I allowed myself a cynical smile. Publicity could also be a severe handicap, as I knew very well. Three years ago, when I'd been preparing to mount an exhibit on Egyptian burial customs, our registrar had been murdered—bashed on the head and stuffed in a sarcophagus. Reporters had made our lives miserable by camping out in the parking lot and pouncing on us whenever we showed our faces.

The steel cables creaked again as the heavy statue began its descent.

Victor stepped into the elevator shaft and looked up. "This should make a good shot," he said, motioning to the video tech. The elevator light gleamed on his distinguished sweep of dark hair touched with gray. The cameraman, standing just outside the shaft for a better angle, pointed his camcorder up. Ellen moved closer and craned her neck.

"Victor!" said Susie, who had the boss' ear at most times since they were a couple both in and out of regular business hours. He looked back at her indulgently as she put a hand on his sleeve. "Don't you think we ought to—"

What Susie thought was never revealed, because the left side of the platform suddenly tilted.

The Emperor Augustus hurtled down, crashing against the side of the shaft as he went. Victor, Susan, and Ellen vanished in a maelstrom of smashed plaster. There was a bone-jarring thud... then an awful silence.

I'd shut my eyes involuntarily and my mouth and nostrils were choked with dust. As I blinked and rubbed my face with both hands, Susie's scream rushed up and down the scale like a tornado siren. The dust lifted.

Victor's crumpled upper body was partially hidden under the wreck of the cable car and chunks of plaster.

One dead museum director.

Two

Same morning

Susie crouched next to Victor's body, sobbing and moaning. I wasn't in much better shape—my knees were shaking like Santa's bowl full of jelly—but I managed to reach over and pat her back.

Susie hardly noticed. "Aieee—Oh, no—Oh, my God! Victor, you can't leave me."

I leaned against the wall, averting my eyes from the pool of blood seeping out from under the biggest piece of statue. How was I going to get Susie away from Victor?

Ellen, her face as white as the plaster of Augustus' flesh, picked herself up off the floor and staggered over to help me. "Susie, come over here. You need to move out of the way." Gently we disentangled her trembling hands from their clutch on Victor's shirt and steered Susie out of the elevator. Susie slid down into a crouch and buried her red curls in her hands.

Dean Saltonstall, a slight, dapper man with short, white hair, sprang into action. After sending George to phone for an ambulance, he steered the reporters out of earshot. I didn't envy him; he'd have a tough time minimizing this tradgedy.

"Dylan Luneau! Get down here at once!"

Yikes. That bellow hardly resembled the Dean's usual measured tones.

Dylan dashed into view, barely out of breath from running down three flights of stairs. A pair of pliers and work gloves peeked out of one of the pockets of his tool belt. "I don't know what happened, Victor..." he panted apologetically.

Ellen said, "Victor can't hear you, Dylan."

Dylan froze as he took in the awful scene. "Oh, shit..."

Ellen reached out a hand to Dylan but he ignored it.

I looked at Dean Saltonstall's face. It was a rigid mask and his eyes had darkened from hazel to brown. Was he wondering, as I was, whether people in our museum were just a little too accident-prone? It was scarcely three years since our last dead body.

"Ms. Perkins, are you all right?" the Dean asked Ellen.

She nodded.

Saltonstall turned to me. "Ms. Donahue? You're uninjured, thank goodness. I want you to phone Detective Sergeant McEwan at the Boston Police Department. Tell him we'd like to consult with him as soon as possible. I'll take care of contacting the University Police."

"Okay." I took the stairs to the fourth floor where my office was. I could see only one silver lining in this situation—McEwan was the best in the homicide business. We'd be in good hands.

~ * ~

Ninety long minutes later, I sat at the huge, scarred wooden table and waited for Saltonstall to start the proceedings. My knees had stopped trembling, but any attempt to think felt like wading through Jell-O.

I glanced around our meeting room. The furniture was as haphazard as the images flitting through my brain. The big table—actually two tables pushed together—was flanked by mismatched chairs gleaned from Surplus Furniture on the other side of campus. Battered file cabinets filled one wall, and the décor was completed by the sort of metal shelving most people reserve for their garages or wood shops, stuffed with used archaeology and history books donated by retiring Classics professors. My colleagues roamed around the room, all of them in various degrees of upset and confusion.

"When are the police arriving?" said Ellen, as she shoved more chairs close to the table.

"Any minute now," Dylan said. He leaned back in a cracked brown leather chair, balancing precariously on two of the four legs. "God, what a mess! How on earth are we going to complete the move now? This place will be full of police and photographers."

I dimly registered the commotion as I latched on to Dylan's question. *How, indeed?* Our staff members were halfway through moving all the collections to a spiffy new building—the Edward G. Taylor Museum, named after a generous donor who'd made his pile managing a Boston bank—on the other side of campus. All but two galleries of the old museum had been closed to the public for six months, and no one except for the senior staff had known we were moving statues this week. Because of the huge amount of labor needed to pack and move fifty thousand artifacts, we'd had a kaleidoscope of temporary staff, students, and volunteers working since the summer. Only Victor—and now presumably Susie—knew how many people had been hired and fired since August. With so many people and objects involved, it wasn't surprising we'd had minor accidents such as two sprained ankles and a broken Roman glass vase. But nothing like this.

Sergeant Bruce McEwan and another cop arrived, followed by the Dean. McEwan was a stocky, middle-aged man who radiated authority. He hadn't changed a bit. His graying eyebrows shot up when he saw me looking at him.

Ellen, who was seated to my right, said hello in a thin little voice. Susie barely acknowledged McEwan's presence. Her green-shadowed eyes fixed steadily on the wall in front of her.

Dylan Luneau inched his chair closer to Ellen, a tacit acknowledgment that they were a couple. His tense shoulders meant that he was dying for a cigarette.

My gaze moved on to my least favorite staff member. George Skirvin slumped dejectedly in a chair at the other end of the table. His whole attitude cried, "I'm an underpaid, overworked student living on junk food—kick me."

Nancy Phelan, our new registrar, and assistant curator Tim Marsden arrived last. Nancy sported dark curly hair, currently rather rumpled, and her eyes were black pools of shock. Tim, a taciturn graduate student from Art History, hid behind floppy brown hair and glasses.

"I'm Detective Sergeant Bruce McEwan and this is Detective Specialist Richards." McEwan motioned to the tall skinny cop on his right. "Let's start with where everyone was just before the Fall of Augustus."

His quip made me smile in spite of myself. Did Sergeant McEwan read Roman history when he wasn't on homicide duty? I wouldn't put it past him.

McEwan waved his ballpoint pen "Richards, sit over next to the door." He glanced around. "Where is Mr. Dylan Luneau?"

"Right here," Dylan said.

"Tell us exactly what you saw and heard before the statue fell."

I was a little surprised that McEwan was conducting a group interview before grilling us individually, but doubtless he had his reasons.

Dylan described how he'd attached the cables the night before. He'd checked the clamps this morning before he sent George downstairs. "I can't believe the statue fell. It doesn't make any sense," he said, looking warily at McEwan.

McEwan's overly dramatic response startled all of us. "Explain this," he said, throwing a section of cable on the table.

I stared. The end of the cable wasn't ragged. It was clean, as if it had been severed—deliberately.

"What the hell?" Dylan said. He shoved one hand through his brown hair.

"I don't believe it," said Ellen, white-faced again. She leaned closer to Dylan as though he might protect her from unpleasantness.

Poor Ellen. Dylan couldn't care less how she was feeling—he was too busy thinking about saving his own skin.

McEwan and his partner watched our reactions carefully. "The cable parted." he told us. "Either it was cut, or someone loosened the bolt that tightened the clamp around the looped end of the cable."

So it was murder, I thought with a mental groan. Why couldn't I work in an ordinary museum, where the worst thing that could happen was the mislabeling of artifacts?

My brain reluctantly shifted into investigative gear. Could Dylan have missed seeing the altered cable, if he were innocent? In the dim light of Wigglesworth Hall, anything was possible. If it weren't Dylan, who would do such a thing? Did the culprit want general mayhem, or was he—or she—intent on killing or maiming a specific victim? And how could he be sure the right victim would be in the right place when Augustus fell?

It was certainly the first time I'd ever thought of a Roman statue as a weapon of destruction.

"Whatever happened to that cable, it didn't happen while I was there," Dylan said, as his neck turned red.

But what if he'd left the area to go to the men's room, or out for a smoke? Or maybe Dylan had done it himself. He had an M.A. in Museum Studies and was completing a PhD in anthropology. Perhaps he thought he was overqualified for his current position and was after Victor's job.

Aha—Dylan was making a sketch of the cable assembly for McEwan. I stood up so I could bend over the table. The diagram showed four cables, each one fastened to a corner of the platform by passing the cable ends through metal eyes. Each loop was then pressed together with a clamp and tightened with a nut and bolt. Dylan and George had gotten the hardware and complete instructions from Operations and Maintenance—surely those guys knew what they were doing. But there was no guarantee the hardware was new; it was much more likely that it was recycled from another use, like most of the furniture in this part of campus.

McEwan rubbed his eleven-o'clock shadow. "Okay, Mr. Luneau. We'll take your diagram for further study. Now, did you take any breaks during your set-up for the statue move?"

"Well, Ellen brought me a cup of coffee, and I may have stepped out for a minute," Dylan said sheepishly.

Great, I thought as I sat down again. Then it could be anyone. Since the building was used for classes as well as for the fourth floor museum and offices for the Departments of Sociology and Psychology, dozens of people passed through the hallways during the day.

McEwan raised one inquisitive eyebrow at Susie. "Miss Blake?"

"I was in and out, checking on things, so I could tell Victor when we were all ready," she said shakily, her baby-blue eyes tearing up again.

"Miss Perkins?"

"After I took Dylan his coffee, I was in the lab until Lisa came to fetch me. Our post was on the first floor, at the bottom of the shaft." Ellen's expression was carefully blank.

McEwan continued around the table, pinpointing where each of us had been during the morning. Just before he got to me, my stomach rumbled loudly. I looked around, pretending the uncouth noise came from someone else, but the Sergeant's sardonic smile made it clear he knew who was guilty.

"Mrs. Donahue-Barber," he said, startling me by using my married name and laying a little stress on the "Mrs." James Barber and I had been married a year and a half now, but there was no reason for McEwan to have kept up with the museum's romances.

"I was at the elevator entrance on the first floor, with Ellen. I heard George's and Dylan's voices from above." I paused. "I didn't actually see anyone because the platform inside the elevator blocked my view."

And Susie? Where had she been at that point in time?

My thoughts scurried around like hungry squirrels while McEwan asked who had been in the building the night before. Answer: everyone, since we were behind schedule on the move. I wondered if McEwan realized that we were all quite used to working at night and on weekends; museums attracted young professionals who were dedicated, manic, and decidedly masochistic.

McEwan asked, "Mrs. Donahue-Barber, can you think of any former employee who may have had a grudge against Dr. Fitzgerald?"

"Well, we did have one young guy last May who was pretty upset when he was fired. What was his name, Susie?"

"Harry. Harold Weinberger. But I haven't seen him around recently." Susie wiped her eyes and sat up straighter.

No one else had either.

McEwan made a note. "I'll need the details on Mr. Weinberger. Miss Blake, you're in charge of keeping records for all employees, right?"

Susie nodded.

"Have there been any other incidents—stuff I should know about?" asked McEwan.

No incidents, I reflected as I watched the sly glances around the table. Just tangled relationships that would surely surface as McEwan investigated. Such as Dylan's love affair with Ellen, which I heartily disapproved of, and Susie's long-term dalliance with Victor. And Dylan's flirtations with every other female on the staff.

"Right," McEwan said. "Detective Richards and I'll be interviewing each of you in turn." He examined his watch. "We'll start with Mr. Luneau, then Mr. Skirvin. The rest of you, you can grab some lunch but don't leave the building." He motioned to a crime scene technician who'd been waiting in the hall to set up his fingerprint kit at a nearby desk. "The elevator shaft will be closed for at least a few days while we investigate. You'll have to use the stairs. That's all for now." His lips tightened as he snapped his notebook shut.

Lunch? The idea of food now, with Victor lying dead, made me queasy. On the other hand, I'd skipped breakfast and didn't see how I could survive a police interrogation without something to fortify me.

Chairs screeched as everyone stood. I collared Ellen and said, "Susie looks awful. Let's order something hot—I can't face the PB&J sandwich and orange I brought today."

Ellen grimaced at the idea of peanut butter. "Okay. Don't know if I can eat anything, but guess I should try. How about Chinese? There's that new place on Commonwealth Ave."

"I'm not that hungry, either, but I could manage some soup and maybe an egg roll. Want to phone in an order for delivery since we're not supposed to leave the building? Meet you in my office."

As I herded Susie down the hall, I spared a thought for James. James wouldn't be exactly thrilled to hear about another murder at my workplace. Normally, he was the most supportive of husbands, but he'd discourage me from any amateur detecting if he thought it would put me in danger. He might even try to persuade me to quit my job.

That would be awkward, because I had no intention of leaving the museum.

~ * ~

My desk was a stratagraphic nightmare that urgently needed excavation. I removed one stratum of papers from my most comfortable seat, an orange-upholstered swivel chair inherited from Sociology, and gently nudged Susie to sit down. Susie drooped like a partially stuffed laundry bag, her eyes still glistening with tears. I scrounged up two more chairs and cleared a space on my desk for the carry-out food.

Ellen appeared with a large bag in record time.

"Wow, that was fast," I said.

"They weren't busy, and I met the delivery boy at the front door," she explained, doling out soup containers, egg rolls, and napkins.

I leaned over to touch Susie's head, forcing her to look up. "Susie. Hey. We know you're in shock, but you've got to eat something. The police want to interview all of us this afternoon, and it won't do to have you faint."

Susie groaned dismally.

I decided a little brutality was in order. "You need your strength, Susie. You know McEwan is going to ask you about your relationship with Victor."

That did it. Susie started to cry again. "Victor—oh, God, he's dead." She covered her face with both hands. "I was going to marry him after the Grand Opening in June; I had my dress all picked out."

Interesting. Ellen's raised eyebrows showed it was news to her, too. Maybe even Victor had been ignorant of Susie's intentions.

Ellen moved her chair so she and I were flanking Susie, and pushed Susie's styrofoam bowl closer to the weeping woman.

The fragrant steam did what no words could accomplish. Susie stopped crying, and picked up her spoon. After two bites of hot-and-sour heaven and a swallow of green tea, she looked gratefully at us. "Thanks. You're right, Lisa. I have to talk to McEwan."

Relieved that Susie was coming around, I took a big crunchy bite of my egg roll. Mmm—pork and cabbage, with little bits of carrot and bean sprouts. Ellen dipped hers in spicy yellow mustard and gagged as her sinuses caught on fire.

"McEwan will want all our personnel records. And Victor's papers. But..." Susie sat up straighter, her eyes wide. "Who's going to run the museum now?"

My stomach clenched as we looked at each other. I pushed my unfinished egg roll aside. Surely the move could be completed without Victor, but there was the Grand Opening to plan, invitations to send out, Deans to placate...

"You're the one who knows how the administrative system works," said Ellen to Susie.

"Yeah, but the Dean will want a PhD. in charge," Susie said. "You know, to interact with faculty and the designers." They both looked at me; my current title was Senior Curator, but I was the only PhD currently on the staff—now.

A shiver of apprehension—or was it anticipation?—ran up my back.

Susie was right—the Dean would want someone with a doctorate to take over, and Susie and Ellen only had M.A. degrees. Could I handle such an appointment? Probably, but like Indiana Jones, I'd have to crawl through a snake pit: the wrath of worried donors, the inflated ego of the architect from New York, the shock and grief of the Museum Friends group.

"Don't look at me that way," I said. "Saltonstall has a mind of his own—he's perfectly capable of conscripting an Interim Director from Anthropology or Classics. Then we'd all have to figure out how to work under someone who doesn't know beans about our museum."

"Sounds like a recipe for disaster," Ellen said.

"We've already had the disaster," Susie replied, looking like she was about to dissolve into tears again.

Detective Richards stuck his head in the door. "Miss Blake, we'd like to talk with you next."

Susie rose reluctantly.

Richards pinned me with an inscrutable gaze.

"You're next," he said, leading Susie away.

Three

Monday, January 13
Same morning

    I limped into Victor's office where McEwan and Richards were waiting for me. My right knee ached from the awkward twisting it had received when I'd dodged the falling statue. I avoided looking at the empty chair behind the desk where Victor usually lounged, elegantly shod feet crossed. I slid awkwardly into the third chair at the conference table and faced my inquisitors.

    I'd been helpful to the police three years ago, when they'd accepted me as an ally once they'd ruled out my involvement in the murder of our registrar. But this was a new case, a new murder, and as I knew very well, that meant I was a suspect until proven innocent, or elsewhere, at the critical time.

    McEwan's dark brown eyes assessed me coolly. His craggy face looked as stern as a stranger's until he smiled. "Well, Mrs. Donahue-Barber, here we are again." To his partner he added, "This is the lady I was telling you about—she assisted us in the last museum murder."

Richards nodded, his thoughtful gray eyes never leaving my face.

"Richards has some experience in art-related crimes, but he's working Homicide now," McEwan said to me. "Okay, Lisa, why don't you take us through your movements last night and this morning."

So far, so good. It looked like he was going to treat me as an ally again. I described how everyone had worked late the night before.

"Can you remember what time everyone left?" McEwan asked.

"I was here until ten," I said. "Ellen stayed after me to close up. I'm not sure what order the others left in—oh, I remember, Tim had to go pick up his mother at the airport just before I left. Say about nine forty-five."

I rubbed my forehead as I thought about what to say next. A headache was starting behind my eyebrows—probably another reaction to the trauma of Victor's death. Not to mention thinking one of my colleagues must be a murderer.

"And today?" McEwan prompted.

"Susie opened the museum this morning—that's normally at eight o'clock. I arrived at nine, give or take five minutes."

McEwan reviewed his notes. "Tim is Timothy Marsden, graduate student? What does he do?"

I nodded. "He's sort of a general assistant, mostly with research and curatorial stuff. But all our job roles have morphed and expanded since the move to the new building started."

"Where was Tim when the statue fell?"

I frowned. "Upstairs, somewhere."

"Did you hear his voice?"

"No, not that I recall."

"You said earlier that you heard Dylan Luneau and George Skirvin's voices above you just before Augustus fell, is that right?"

"Yes."

"What about Susan Blake?"

"I'm not sure where Susie was when I heard Dylan's voice the first time, but she was certainly on the first floor when Victor and the Dean appeared."

"Did she come from the same direction as Victor, or from the opposite stairway?"

"The north stairs." I remembered Susie's chirpy comment about museum publicity.

"Did you observe the cable after it broke?"

"No, not until you brought it into the staff meeting. I thought it looked cut. It's a braided steel rope, right?"

"That's right," McEwan said, lifting his eyebrows.

He shouldn't have looked so surprised; paying attention to materials was part of a curator's training.

He showed me a sketch—his own, not Dylan's—in his notebook. "See, the cable goes through the eye of this metal piece and is supposed to be clamped in two places. A separate piece of metal forms the clamp, which is tightened with bolts and nuts. One bolt is missing."

I examined the diagram, thinking anyone could have loosened the cable assembly if he or she had the right tool. But I couldn't explain the severed end of the cable.

"Yup. Anyone could have done it," he said, reading my mind. "Anyone with access to tools and a little time alone. I assume your staff members have tools lying around?"

I described the museum toolboxes I knew about—the one in the workshop downstairs, and the one in the gallery storage area on the fourth floor.

"Hmm." He made a note. "We're pretty sure what happened here, but we're sending the cable assembly off for analysis to make sure."

"If the cable was mostly cut through, that would have to be done in advance, right?"

"Yeah. Even with the right tool, it'd take time to cut through that kind of wire. Then the cable would have to be reattached to the platform in such as way that no one would notice it couldn't bear the full weight of the statue. We don't have any proof of tampering—yet." McEwan switched gears. "What kind of boss was Dr. Fitzgerald?"

"A very good one," I answered, surprising myself. "Efficient, fair, thoughtful…" Nothing like my first museum boss, Valerie Albrecht, the Director from Hell. "He gave each of us a chance to prove ourselves, without micromanaging. And he had a knack for inclusive leadership; he listened to our opinions, encouraged discussion, and then made decisions."

"So you liked him."

"Yes. He was a difficult person to know well—quite reserved, really—but I did like him." A lump rose in my throat as I realized how much I would miss him; we all would. My head now felt like a jackhammer was inside it.

McEwan stared at my forehead as if he could see the pain inside. "Did you ever lust after his job?" he asked.

I stiffened. "You mean, enough to drop a statue on him?"

Good grief, he couldn't really think that was a possibility!

"I am ambitious," I said firmly, "but not enough to kill people in my way! Besides, I have a very good understanding of what a Director's job entails. Too much placating administrators and entertaining donors for me. Being Senior Curator is just fine—I've got enough responsibility to make me feel challenged, but I still have occasional stints in the library when I can bury myself in old books." I wasn't being entirely truthful—I did fantasize sometimes about how I'd run the museum if I ever got the chance.

"Just asking," McEwan said with a little smile.

Damn the man. It was his job to be inquisitive, but I'd always had the distinct feeling that he enjoyed baiting me. "Sure."

"Remember, I have to consider all possible motives."

I glared at him. "Remember how much I helped you last time? We're supposed to be allies here."

"Cool it, Ms. Donahue." McEwan's eyes lost their warmth and his mouth tightened.

"Miss Blake told us that Dr. Fitzgerald was going to fire George Skirvin," said Detective Richards in a smooth tenor voice. "Did you know anything about that?"

"No, I had no idea. Did Susie say why?"

"He was incompetent," McEwan said. "Apparently, your ex-boss was giving him one more chance—another month to see if he could shape up." He looked at his notes. "Tell us about Skirvin's background."

"Well, he's an undergrad Anthro—I mean, Anthropology—major, new to the museum this semester. He works primarily for Dylan, but we all ask him for help occasionally." I knew McEwan wanted to know about George's personality. "He's difficult: always complaining people are picking on him. The sort who's never satisfied and generally behaves obnoxiously."

"Not your favorite colleague?"

I shook my head. "He's a nasty little twerp."

McEwan lips twitched at my sudden descent into informality. "Okay, what about Dylan Luneau?"

"He's not my favorite, either," I said, choosing my words carefully. "Dylan's good at his job—he's the preparator for all the exhibits, and in charge of all the packing of artifacts for our move. He often irritates me."

"Oh?"

"He's too smooth," I blurted. "He acts like he knows everything already, doesn't need direction from anyone, and he's like the Pied Piper with the younger women on the staff."

Especially my best friend, Ellen, who made the mistake of moving in with him.

"And he blow-dries and gels his hair," McEwan said, as if that were the worst offense a man could commit. He flipped his notebook shut. "I need to interview the other staff, but I'll come back to you. I'm counting on you to keep your eyes open, Lisa." His use of my first name reassured me. "That means don't go sticking your nose into things—just observe and report."

Yeah. Telling me not to snoop was like wiggling a pencil under a newspaper in front of a bored kitten.

"I'll tell you if I notice anything."

In my own good time.

Four

Same day, late afternoon

James Barber was working his butt off.

At Beth Israel Deaconess Hospital, a pile-up on the Southeast Expressway during the morning rush hour had thrown off the schedules in most departments.

James circled his shoulders to try and loosen up his muscles. He'd already read twenty-five X-rays and CT scans from accident victims, with many more to come. It didn't help that the new patient record system was down—again—so everyone was backed up on data entry.

The phone rang. Charlie Sloan. "Hey, James—you seen your buddy José?" Charlie Sloan's booming bass voice gave no clue that he was only five feet ten and slimly built. Charlie was one of the good guys—a mature person, not just an overgrown teenager with an inflated sense of entitlement. So many of the physicians expected the world handed to them on a platter, but Charlie understood that you had to earn the high salary and generous vacation with years of hard work. And Charlie shared James' interest in photography, so they always had a lot to talk about.

"No, why?"

"He took off on an errand to the morgue a while back, and we really need him. We have a zillion slides to prepare, and a lot of gross specimens to cut."

James was not surprised. José was a dedicated worker, but he was courting a girl who worked in the hospital cafeteria. "If I see him, Charlie, I'll tell him to get his ass back up there."

"Thanks. Hey, when this madness is over, I'm going to do the autopsy on the Gillespie case—remember? The one with the shadow on the liver that showed up in X-ray?"

"Yeah, I'd like to see that. I'd really like to know if it was a metastasis or not."

"Will do. Oh, and next time you're up here, I'll show you my new lens."

"Okay."

James glanced at his watch. Four-thirty. He realized he'd skipped lunch; he was starving and in dire need of caffeine. He could get a snack and look for José at the same time. James pulled on his white coat and clattered down the stairs. As he navigated the hall with its tan-painted walls and dim lighting, he passed a metal cart bearing a burden—a dead body discreetly shrouded with a green tarp.

José often hinted about various unsavory activities that took place in the basement of the hospital where far too many people had access. Tunnels lined with storerooms connected the fifty-year old building with the clinic across the street. The best hideaway was the morgue suite with its alcove of rooms, equipped with bathroom, lockers, benches, table, and sink—a perfect rendezvous for couples, people wanting a private smoke away from the smoke-free hospital public areas, maybe drug deals.

The morgue itself was a long, narrow room, hardly bigger than the freshman dorm room James had shared with a roommate. Instead of bunk beds, it featured a stainless steel table with a sink and an organ-dissection platform. Another sink that looked like a toilet huddled against the far wall, and pipes for disposing of bodily fluids and waste water ran everywhere. The morgue's only interior decorations were the blackboard with organ weights and a bulletin board with official notices. On the counter lurked jars of pickled organs floating in formaldehyde. James' nose wrinkled as it absorbed the sickly-sweet odor.

Dr. Michael "Mic" Andrews lifted his autopsy knife out of a vat of disinfectant. Unlike dapper Charlie, Mic was a beefy guy, with blond hair going gray and an incipient paunch. A bit pompous, he made sure everyone knew he was a Harvard graduate. He boasted about his decorative wife, who spent all his money redecorating their posh suburban home in Wellesley, and complained about the bills generated by his two private-schooled teenagers.

"Hi, Mic. Seen José? Charlie Sloan's looking for him."

Mic slid a new disposable blade into the huge knife. "Not today. He's often down here checking the slide archives in the annex, though." Mic grinned cheerfully, as if he were at a cocktail party instead of in the grim setting of death and dissection.

James didn't return the smile. He tried to stay on good terms with his colleagues, but he just couldn't warm up to this guy. And Mic was resisting changes James had proposed in the last Quality Assurance meeting.

James nodded at the skinny *diener*, Steven Trendall, grateful that he wasn't the one moving patients in and out of the cooler. Even with the help of a sinister hook-and-chain apparatus on a wheeled frame, the body now being hoisted looked like a five-hundred-pounder.

"Bad business, this accident. Maybe we wouldn't have had such a pileup if it were May instead of January. All the roads were slick this morning," said James.

"Yeah, but you know Boston drivers. Weather makes no difference; they were born crazy," said Mic.

James laughed. "Know what you mean. They dip and dive around other cars without so much as a horn toot. Not like down south. When I did a rotation in North Carolina, I noticed southern drivers do stupid things at the speed of tortoises—they wait until you're almost level with them, then they ease out slowly right in front of you."

"I think I'd prefer slow southern drivers," said Mic. He turned to Steven Trendall. "My back is killing me. Help me shift the next one onto the table."

Trendall's arm muscles corded as he maneuvered the hoist over the table, lowered the body, and then heaved it into position. He must work out, thought James. Or else his *diener* job—moving bodies around and assisting with autopsies—was enough to keep him in shape.

"Too bad we don't have a bigger cooler," said Steven in a nasal twang. "Or a drying room. Then we could desiccate the tissues so the organs wouldn't fall apart when you cut 'em..."

"Hell, no! I don't want bodies stored here!" said Mic. "That's why we ship them out to funeral homes for embalming."

"Yeah, but it would be so cool to treat the bodies here. See, the ancient Egyptians used *natron*, a special kind of salt..."

Whoa, another mummy enthusiast, thought James. He must remember to tell Lisa. His wife had an abiding interest in everything to do with Egyptian mummification.

He left the morgue, almost tripping over a couple of body bags awaiting Dr. Andrews's delicate attentions. He passed a janitor taking a break in a tiny, box-like office used by the housekeeping and janitorial staff. It had a small fridge and a coffee maker, but James thought it was a bleak sort of place to sit when you could go upstairs into the sky-lit lobby. Still, it was one more example of an out-of-the-way place to hide in the bowels of the hospital. Remembering his original errand, James stopped in the basement cafeteria and grabbed a ham sandwich and a coffee. As he was standing at the cashier's station, he spotted José seated at a small table with a cute, dark-haired young woman in a light blue uniform.

He walked over and nudged his friend. "I know you've got important business down here with Vicki, but Charlie Sloan's looking for you."

José looked at his watch. "Damn! I meant to keep my break short. Thanks, Barber."

James nodded and headed back to Radiology. Before he was halfway up the stairs, his beeper went off. Pulling it off his belt clip, he saw that his office was trying to reach him. He exited at the first door and found a hall phone.

"Dr. Barber here. What's the problem, Delia?"

"Dr. Stanton called from OR3—he has a Mr. George Bielaski who's scheduled for surgery in an hour. He's a prior cardiac case so they need his film X-rays to compare to today's set, and no one can find them. He wants to talk to you."

James groaned. "Fine, put me through." Stanton was his least favorite cardiac surgeon, a Type A personality with a huge ego who wanted everything STAT.

"Barber, what is it with your department? We've got a patient here who needs immediate surgery and I can't find his goddamn X-rays! And this isn't the first time this has happened..."

James put on his best diplomatic voice. "I'm sure the older films are in transit—you know it's a madhouse today with all these accident victims. I will personally look into it and call you right back."

"Do that! And don't let it happen again!" Stanton hung up.

Sighing, James slipped the beeper back on his belt. What he really wanted to say was that any previously scheduled elective surgery should wait until the accident victims were taken care of, but Stanton was the sort of surgeon who thought his patients came first even during a blizzard when his staff couldn't make it into the hospital.

As he trudged up the last flight of stairs, James thought about the joys of being a department head during a computer software transition of this magnitude. Radiology had just adopted a software program, Virtual Man, for digital storage of X-rays and CT scans. New, digital images were easy to access—except on days when the program had glitches—but they still had to be compared to the older, film images kept in the vault for patients with prior histories. So the old system of sending large envelopes of film around the hospital was still in place, with all its potential for delay and misplacement.

When mix-ups occurred on the same day that the patient record system was down, no one could locate anything and tempers grew short.

Shedding his white coat, James plunked himself down in front of his monitor. As he picked up the phone to make the first of several calls to locate the missing X-rays, he scanned the list of new digital images in his VirtMan inbox.

Fifteen new ones. A big eyestrain day, despite the spiffy new monitor and high resolution images. James rolled up the sleeves of his blue shirt and opened the first file.

~ * ~

By six p.m., James had reached the point of no return: if he read any more X-rays—digital or film—tonight, he'd start missing things. And early morning was the right time for writing his planned memo about better tracking of film X-rays with the right blend of authority and diplomacy. Time to go home.

He preferred to walk since he spent most of his day cooped up in the underground levels of Deaconess Hospital. The pungent smells of Boston—bus exhaust, salt water, and old fish—were infinitely preferable to the hospital stinks of disinfectant and fear.

James turned right onto their side street, past the Brookline Food Market, navigating piles of frozen slush and un-scooped, partially thawed dog poop that lazy dog owners refused to pick up. He hoped that Lisa and the kids would be late; it would be sheer luxury to have the house to himself for a few minutes. He'd sip a Dunkelweiss and read the paper before the others arrived. Maybe he'd even start dinner.

"Hello! I'm home!" He let the door slam and waited. The antique wood and enamel clock ticked loudly on the mantelpiece. No human answered his call, but a streak of black-and-white lightning tore through the flap in the door from the basement. Oreo, Lisa's cat, had been cooped up all day and was ready to play.

"Hang on a minute, chum, and let me get settled." James and the cat were gradually coming to an understanding. Lisa was still the primary cat slave, but Oreo knew he could wheedle occasional treats and good wrestling matches out of James.

Feeling virtuous, he found the casserole Lisa had prepared for tonight and popped it into a three-fifty degree oven. Then James kicked off his shoes, popped off the lid of his beer, and stretched his long body out on the couch. Now for the paper. He opened it unsuspectingly.

Pounce.

Oreo's perfect, twenty-point landing was right in the middle of the Boston Globe's front page. "Why, you little monster," said James, sitting up again. He tickled the cat's plush white tummy, and Oreo wrapped all four paws around his hand and dug in with his needle-sharp claws.

They had just completed a satisfactory tussle without too much of James's blood getting on the paper when he heard a key in the lock and a commotion at the back door.

Nine-year old Sam sped into the living room. "Daddy!"

"How was school?"

"Okay, I guess." Sam hid his face in James's shirt and butted him like a much younger child.

James hugged his son and tousled his dark hair, and then captured Emma, who was rushing around in little circles, her jacket flapping.

"I'm a hawk! I'm a hawk!" she cried.

James grinned at her as he remembered that Emma's class was in the middle of a bird-watching unit.

He kissed his wife. Then he stood back and took a closer look at her haggard face. "What's wrong?"

"Plenty. Wait 'till I get the kids a snack." Quickly Lisa dug out some cheese and an open box of Wheat Thins. Sam and Emma homed in on the food like little vultures.

"Upstairs, guys," she said, handing the plate to Emma. "I'll call you when dinner's ready."

The kids rushed up the stairs to their third floor den and the TV.

"Bad day at the office?"

"You could say that." Lisa sagged against the counter, too weary even to shrug off her coat and kick off her boots. Her long blond braid was untidy and her blue eyes cloudy and unfocused. "My boss was killed today—by a falling statue. And it looks like the cable holding the statue was deliberately cut."

James gulped air. "*Victor Fitzgerald is dead?*"

"Yup. Crushed by the Roman emperor Augustus."

James realized her flippant tone was a symptom of shock. Gently, he removed her coat from her unresponsive shoulders and nudged her towards a chair. "Sit." He opened the fridge and got out the Yellow Tail Chardonnay Lisa preferred and poured her a glass. "Now tell me."

Lisa did, leaving nothing out.

"So who did it?"

"I don't know. Most of us liked Victor. He was severe, but very fair." Her blue eyes filled with tears. "You know I had my problems with him when I was a new employee—"

"That was because you weren't used to his management style."

"Yeah, and he was relatively new then, too." She wiped her wet cheeks with one sleeve. "McEwan asked me lots of questions about the staff—personality quirks, how they relate to each other—but I think the real problem in solving this one will be motive."

"You mean, Victor wasn't disliked enough to be murdered, unlike your old boss Val?"

"Yeah. He's—was—a pussycat compared to her."

James's green eyes hardened. "Your role is passive observation, not active sleuthing, right, honey?"

She smiled wanly and kept her mouth shut.

James regarded her with skepticism. He wanted to believe that his wife had learned from past experience that messing around with a murder investigation wasn't a healthy occupation for an amateur. Last time, she'd nearly been brained by a vase-wielding maniac. But she wasn't talking; that meant she was already hard at work considering means, motive, and opportunity for everyone in the museum.

"Lisa."

"Yes?"

"You're not McEwan's unpaid assistant. Don't let him recruit you."

"All he wants me to do is—"

"No!"

"You can't tell me to be blind and dumb! McEwan wants me to observe and report—that's all." Her blue eyes resembled ice chips.

James stared at his wife. When they'd first met, he'd admired Lisa's spunk and independence. Then, when he fell in love, he learned how to worry about her. He sighed. "I know I can't tell you what to do, Lisa. But I can ask, can't I? To please keep yourself safe, for the children's sake, if not for mine?"

There was a long silence.

"I can't make Victor's murder not have happened. I'm involved whether I like it or not. But I will do my very best to stay out of trouble. Okay?"

James wished he could wrap her up in cotton wool—or drag her off to a nice, safe cave. "Okay—for now." He stepped behind her and began to massage her neck and shoulders.

Five

Tuesday, January 14

The smooth red-and-black pottery winked and gleamed under the fluorescent lights. I hunched over the table, clutching a yellow pad of paper and pretending to compose my wall texts and artifact labels. My brain wasn't working. The inside of my head felt as clogged as a saucepan full of cold, congealed oatmeal. And of course I'd slept badly, tortured by memories of the day before.

Red pottery, red blood... falling statues... Susie crying.

"Earth and Fire," my exhibit on ancient ceramic technology would open in five weeks. I was nowhere near ready and fresh out of ideas. I grabbed my black cat mug and gulped some tepid, brain-restoring coffee.

Focus! I told myself.

Greek firing technology—that was the key to the this part of the exhibit, since the beehive-shaped kiln had enabled ancient Greek potters to produce two colors, red and black, on the same vase. The orangey red was the color of the clay fired in an oxidizing atmosphere; the black was a slip made from the same clay, fired in a reducing, or oxygen-poor, atmosphere. The potters used damp wood for smoke and openings in the top of the kiln to regulate the flow of oxygen.

The kiln itself was illustrated on a Corinthian clay plaque, reproduced in countless books on ancient Greek art. I stared at the image in my notebook. James always said it looked like a man feeding a dragon instead of a slave stoking a kiln—and the perspective of the human figure was definitely screwy. It looked like a drawing made by a kindergartener.

Okay, one wall text could be about the firing procedures and the difficulties of controlling time, temperature, and atmosphere to keep the pots from blowing up or cracking. Oh, I could add that great poem about kiln spirits! Spinning my chair around, I groped for my favorite book on vase painting. Where was it? I flipped the pages... aha! This little nugget from the *Life of Homer* would make a lovely introduction to the kiln section:

"If you potters turn shameless and deceitful, then I do summon the ravagers of kilns, Smasher and Crasher and Asbestos (Unquenchable) and Shake-to-pieces and Conqueror of the Unbaked... may the whole kiln be thrown into confusion and the potters loudly wail..."

The passage was perfect; I especially liked it because it conveyed the unpredictable nature of anything connected to fire.

I flipped through Anne Blasingham-Gray's wonderful book, marveling all over again at the records of Greek daily life—both real and imagined—that were preserved in vase paintings. The *tondos* of cups and the outsides of pitchers showed a huge variety: women bathing and preparing for their weddings; drinking *symposia* with dancers, musicians, and wine servers; battle scenes and chariot races; mythological groupings of satyrs, Amazons, giants, and birds with human heads.

The surface treatments were exquisite, rivaling or even surpassing modern ceramics. The polished surface of the amphora in front of me was the result of several hours of careful burnishing, probably by a lowly slave. On the body of the vase was a field of reserved red clay, decorated with black silhouettes of nude male runners with incised muscles and facial features. The delicate rendering of the stomach muscles or the ears provided clues to the identity of the painter—especially helpful when the vase was unsigned. Distinguishing between the work of different vase painters and their apprentices was a whole subspecialty of classical archaeology.

Some vase painters applied a touch of purple for grape vines, and most used white slip for female faces. This vase had no added color, just red clay and black glaze.

Or red blood and white plaster. My fickle brain flashed an image of my dead boss lying on the floor of the elevator, partially covered by the statue of the emperor Augustus.

Why wasn't my brain like a partitioned computer hard drive, so I could push a button and turn off the part I didn't need or want? But how could I ignore a murder in my workplace? I couldn't write wall texts on forming and decorating Greek vases until I'd summarized the crime scene. And made a list of the possible motives and murderous capabilities of my immediate colleagues.

I pulled my pad of paper closer and stared at the runners on the vase again. Hmm. The lead runner's profile looked a bit like Dylan's. Smarmy, self-centered, pseudo-sophisticated Dylan Luneau. I'd held back while talking with McEwan, but I suspected the wily sergeant had picked up on the fact that I thought Dylan was a total jerk. The very same jerk who lived with my best friend, Ellen Perkins.

I wrote down "Dylan: selfish jerk."

Ellen was going to get hurt. Dylan had "womanizer" written all over him, and I'd seen him flirting with Sara Browning. Ellen would probably be dumped for a newer, younger female in six months. But I knew Ellen very well; nothing I could say or do would change the course of this romance. Ellen had a long history of dating men who were bad for her, and each relationship took her through the same emotional stages: infatuation, dawning suspicion, and utter disillusionment. For me, the only real question was whether Dylan's selfish nature masked the kind of supreme ego needed to change him from a jerk into a murderer.

I glanced at the amphora again. The second runner had a bit of a potbelly: George Skirvin, Dylan's downtrodden assistant. Ellen had maliciously nicknamed him "Georgie-Porgie" and it had stuck. I suspected that Georgie knew who'd named him, and resented Ellen accordingly. But Georgie resented almost everyone since he had a victim's personality—everything that happened to him was someone else's doing. He didn't have the guts to take personal responsibility for anything, let alone killing someone.

I scribbled "sulky nerd" next to George's name.

The third nude runner, taller and leaner than the other two, was surely Tim Marsden, loping along behind the others and never catching up. Just like his thesis, which had been "in progress" for four years and counting. Tim was an art historian specializing in the European Iron Age. Victor Fitzgerald, who'd been responsible for acquiring a large collection of early Celtic art, had been his advisor.

The same runner, now dressed in preppy khakis and a polo shirt, suddenly appeared at my elbow. "Lisa? Are you busy? I mean, if you're really busy, I can come back."

I slapped my arm over the list of names on my pad.

Wanting to say, "Hell, yes! Go away!" I said instead, "No, Tim, I'm not busy. I'm supposed to be writing my exhibit texts, but I can't concentrate."

"Know what you mean. Dr. Fitzgerald's death is a terrible thing." He pulled up a chair and straddled it backwards. "Did you have your interview with the cops already?"

"Yep, yesterday morning."

"I just got done talking with Detective McEwan." Tim shifted his backside and re-settled his long legs.

I waited, wondering what was coming next.

"He asked a lot of questions about my relationship with Dr. Fitzgerald. Like, did we get along, did I think he was a good advisor?"

"Well, did you? Get along with Victor, I mean?"

Tim scowled. "He was good, but he was awfully picky. I finished a complete first draft of my thesis six months ago, and Victor was just sitting on it. "

Strange. Victor was usually efficient; he wouldn't have held up Tim's final thesis submission if there'd been nothing wrong with his work. And he'd been an ABD (all but dissertation) for years before I'd arrived at the museum—that usually meant there was a problem, either with the scholarship or the student's ability to finish writing. Maybe I should ask Susie what she knew.

"Did Victor tell you that he wanted revisions?"

"Um, yeah. I rewrote a few sections, which he passed, but then he said I needed to pay more attention to Werner's ideas. I'd already done that in my introduction." Tim shoved his floppy hair off his forehead with one nail-bitten hand and shifted on his chair again. "And he didn't give me a good recommendation for the one-year teaching position at Princeton I applied for."

"How do you know?"

"He said it wasn't the right job for me, but I know it would have been perfect. I'm an academic—I don't want to stay in the museum world forever, I want to be a professor of art history." Tim sounded really aggrieved. "Now I'm a suspect—the cops seem to think I had a motive."

"Well, I don't think you have anything to worry about, Tim."

Unless, of course, you did it.

"Suspicion is one thing," I continued. "They suspect all of us at this point. But they can't arrest anyone without some kind of solid evidence."

"Oh. I hope you're right. I figured you'd know, since you worked with McEwan before."

Oh, swell. Tim was probably not the only staff member to think I had an inside track with the police just because I'd been a valuable witness in a previous murder case.

"I was a suspect then, too, Tim. And Sergeant McEwan hasn't ruled me out this time. The best thing to do is to be cooperative—don't hold anything back. It really looks bad when the cops find out stuff you didn't tell them."

"Okay." He sighed gustily and heaved his long frame out of the chair. "See you later."

I watched Tim slouch away, wondering if he were capable of murdering his advisor. Tim appeared shy initially, but conversations like the one we'd just had revealed his intense, goal-oriented personality. That kind of person was often very good at controlling and disguising his emotions.

It didn't make sense for Tim to kill his advisor, at least not before his thesis was approved and deposited. One could hardly get a PhD in murder. But, of course, there were other advisors—the rest of the committee could still accept the thesis, if they didn't know Tim was a killer.

What about our other staff members?

Susie had loved Victor, and Victor was her ticket to financial and marital security. Scratch Susie as a potential murderess.

Ellen was my best friend. So what if that made me a biased investigator? I refused to consider Ellen as a suspect.

What about Nancy?

The unlabeled vases looked at me reproachfully.

Concentrate, Lisa! Exhibit first, murder later. I turned back to my pots. Too bad I didn't have slaves like the ancient Greeks. Slaves to do all the menial jobs like writing labels and building stands, the modern equivalent of digging the clay, throwing the vases, and stoking the kiln.

Exhaustion overtook me like a Mack truck passing a VW Bug. I slumped forward, rested my weary head on my folded arms, and escaped into snooze-land.

~ * ~

About an hour later, awake and re-caffeinated, I was reviewing my list of vases to illustrate different aspects of the decorating and firing processes when Nancy Phelan sidled into the workroom.

"Lisa, I've pulled the vases for the Roman technology case. Should I line them up on that table, the one you're using?" Her chestnut curls bobbed adorably around her narrow face, but even her bright red turtleneck couldn't make up for her shadowed eyes. Nancy's hero worship for Victor had not died with his death—it was impossible to believe that she'd had anything to do with it.

"That would be great. Let me see." I stood up, stretched, and walked over to the table to help her unload the cart.

"Oh, great, you brought the stamped lamps and the amphora handles as well!" I gazed greedily at a tray of exquisitely molded Roman lamps, *terra sigillata*, and portions of wine jars that would illustrate mass-production in ancient Rome. "Now I can write the wall texts on Roman economy and trade networks with France and Germany."

"You mean some of these ceramics were produced outside Italy?" Nancy said.

"Yes, in Roman outposts in near Lyons and Rheinzabern."

"*Terra sigillata*— that means 'stamped earthenware,' right?" Nancy picked up a delicate bowl stamped with vines and leaves.

"Yep. 'Poor man's silver' is the other name for it. Roman satellite factories produced this for soldiers living abroad who couldn't afford silver and gold. See, the stamped and molded designs imitate the metal originals."

"Huh. Is this a manufacturer's stamp?" She pointed to Roman letters set inside a footprint-shaped stamp.

I peered at it. "I think so, but it's tricky because it could be the factory stamp, the potter's stamp, or the bowl finisher's stamp. I'd have to look it up in Peacock's book."

"Um, Lisa—"

Clearly, she wanted to change the subject. "Yes?"

Nancy fingered the fabric of her black wool skirt. "About Victor. It's hard to believe he's gone. It's so horrible."

I felt guilty that I'd been thinking about anything else. "Indeed, it is horrible."

"Lisa—do you know who's going to be Interim Director?"

"No." Again, I wondered if it would be me, or whether the Dean would hire some professor from outside the University. Or would he look close to home, and choose Dan Grossman from Classics? Or maybe Belinda Feinstein from Anthropology? With the Grand Opening of the new building less than five months away, he couldn't afford to leave us leaderless for very long.

"The thing is..." Nancy's voice was high-pitched, like that of a five-year-old child instead of a twenty-something young woman. With her slight figure and Shirley Temple curls, she certainly didn't look old enough to be married to a physics professor. "...my appointment papers never came though. Victor was going to sign them, and send them over to Personnel, but..."

"You don't know if he actually did it, and whether your job is secure," I finished.

"Right." Nancy's eyes implored me. "If there's anything you can do, I'd really appreciate it. I just love this job." Nancy had been a librarian before she and her husband had moved to Boston, so her transition to being a museum registrar was a natural one. Both jobs required tracking objects and using a database with close attention to detail.

"Sure, Nancy, but you might check with Susie. She handles most of the Personnel stuff."

"I will, but everyone thinks you're going to be the next Director, so I wanted to talk with you." Nancy's mouth curved up in a little smile as she turned away.

I ground my teeth and tugged at my long braid. The attitude of the staff towards me was changing already; I sensed a combination of toadying and deference. Everyone realized the pecking order would change. Would they still confide in me if the Dean made me Director?

Ha, ha.

~ * ~

Later that day, I received a summons from Dean Saltonstall. My heart beating like a wet sneaker tumbling around inside a clothes dryer, I approached his office.

"Lisa, have a seat." Dean Saltonstall came around the desk to sit near me. "Terrible business, this sudden death," he said, avoiding using the term "murder."

"Yes. Victor was a good director; we miss him already." My neck muscles tensed and my hands grew clammy.

"Well, I'm not going to beat around the bush. Victor's death puts us in a very awkward position, what with the new building and all. I'd like you to take over as Interim Director, Lisa, until we can complete a formal search for his replacement. I will raise your salary, of course, and you can put your name in for the permanent job since you have a doctorate..."

His voice faded into the background. I had the sensation of teetering on the edge of a cliff; my life was about to change in ways I couldn't anticipate. Work would get harder—and lonelier. Even my relationship with Ellen was not immune. But my options were limited, and I had no good reason to refuse. And would I really want to work under any one else? The thoughts raced through my head as I tuned back into the Dean's agenda.

"I'm sure I can count on you to tread carefully with the police during their investigation of Victor's untimely demise..."

He might as well call it a murder.

"...and to keep the staff focused on the move," Saltonstall continued.

"I'll do my best," I said.

Looks like you just accepted the job, Lisa!

I sat up straighter. "And I may apply for the permanent position, but I'd like to get a feel for the job first."

"Ah, yes," The Dean appraised me shrewdly. "You have two children now, right?"

"Yes, but they're both in elementary school. That isn't an issue," I said, irritated.

I wished he would focus on my experience and qualifications for the job, not my home life. But Saltonstall was another generation; he was still getting used to female administrators who successfully juggled demanding careers and childrearing. "James is very supportive about childcare emergencies, as much as he can be with his hospital schedule."

"Fine, fine." Dean Saltonstall's glance glided past my head and he checked his watch. He rose to his feet, and I followed his cue.

"Shall I give you a call about the police progress in a day or two?" I asked, moving toward the door.

"Yes, that's a good idea, although I think McEwan will stay in touch."

"What about the Press?"

"Ah." The Dean was clearly impressed that I was already on the job. "If—I should say, when—reporters call you, use the printed release my secretary will give you. Tell them I'm going to give a Press conference tomorrow and try to answer all their questions."

I nodded.

"We'll meet in a week or two to see how things are going. Cooperate fully with the police, and if any donors give you trouble, you can refer them to me."

I walked slowly towards the stairs, thinking if I really wanted to be Director, I'd better show the Dean I could handle tricky donors without his help.

Now that the inevitable had happened, I felt calmer. But where was the sense of elation I'd expected, all those times I'd fantasized about reaching the top of the museum heap? Already, this felt like navigating a Monopoly board stacked with little red hotels and other obstacles.

Museum director at thirty-five—good move, pass Go, collect two hundred dollars.

Director of a museum where a murder had just taken place—bad move, take a Chance card.

Go to Jail.

Six

Same day, evening

Ironically, our entire Donahue-Barber family played Monopoly that night. Sam was obsessed with the game; he really enjoyed fleecing his family. He demonstrated his budding entrepreneurial talents by forcing his parents to pay high rents and hotel rates. Submitting to this outrage was my way of perking him up, since anything connected with school lately seemed to upset him.

"You owe me five hundred, Mom," Sam chortled.

"Guess you'd better pay up," James said, grinning and leaning back against the coffee table.

I fumbled with my play money until I produced four hundred dollar bills and five twenties. "There, you little real estate king—how does it feel to be rich?"

"Great!" Sam eyed the board perched on the imitation Turkish carpet—a Home Depot purchase. "But I need another hotel on Ventnor Ave. so I can get you again when you come around the corner."

"Demon!" Since I was the banker, I accepted Sam's money and handed him another red plastic hotel. Sam's face brightened as he lined the hotel up with the others on his latest piece of property. The game had definitely cheered him.

"My turn!" cried Emma, rolling the dice with a clatter.

I exchanged a smile with James, but I couldn't relax. While the others moved around the board, I gazed at the snow falling outside the living room window and thought about the Stressometer Ellen and I had invented as shorthand for major stress factors in our lives. We'd started with a pop psychology article listing the usual stuff like divorce, losing a job, moving, or a death in the family. Our imaginary gauge measured disasters using temperature in degrees Fahrenheit. We'd embellished the list over the years with conditions like Ellen's propensity for adding a "Toxic Man in Your Life."

Now I could add a few more adverse events from my own life.

Interim museum director during a murder investigation, maybe sixty degrees.

Step-mom to a nine-year old who was suddenly acting like a six year-old, heat up to seventy-five.

Wife to a workaholic doctor who didn't notice that his son was unhappy, at least ninety degrees.

Not as bad as losing a loved one—both James and I had lost a spouse, and that definitely measured over a hundred—but definitely not good. After the past week at the museum, I felt like a juggler who'd just been given one more ball than I could handle; soon I'd lose my grip and the pieces of my life would fly apart.

"Your turn, Mom," said Emma, clasping the knees of her purple sweat pants and rocking back and forth perilously close to the bank. She overbalanced and the money went flying.

"Dad! Look what she did!" cried Sam.

Sam landed on Emma and the two of them rolled around in the wreckage of the board game.

"It's time for bed anyhow," I said, feeling like—and becoming—chief ogre.

"Nooo!"

"Aw, Maawwmm!"

~ * ~

"So, Madam Director, how does it feel to finally be in charge?" James asked me as we collected little green plastic houses and put away the Monopoly game after the children were in bed.

I blew out a long breath. "I thought I would be thrilled if this ever happened, but there's so much going on—"

"You mean, murder and stuff," James said

"That, plus my exhibit coming up, and changes in the staff's attitude."

"How so? You've only had the job for a few hours."

"Well, when I came back from the meeting with Dean Saltonstall, everyone congratulated me, but Dylan and Ellen kind of avoided my eyes, and Susie hardly spoke at all."

"Susie's still in shock, and Ellen's probably realizing that since you're now the boss, you might look less kindly on her relationship with Dylan. Mixing business and pleasure in the workplace is never a good idea, and many bosses frown on or prohibit such behavior. And Ellen's smart enough to know that you'll have to sublimate your relationship as her best friend for the time being. The other staff can't see you playing favorites."

I met his eyes. "That's a good point."

"So what else is bothering you?" asked my perceptive husband.

I hesitated. "I think Sam is finding school difficult. I'm not sure why, but he won't respond when I ask questions about how things are going. And his grades are dropping."

We'd been over this ground before, several times. Sam had been reluctant to move to the new house and give up his old room. Now he was having trouble at school, and James kept playing it down as a normal adjustment to a changed household with a new stepmother and a stepsister.

But I usually made it home before James. I drove the kids home from their after-school program, so I was the first one to hear their daily bulletins. And their jokes, gossip, whining—all vital information to a mom who was trying to keep her finger on the pulse of a recently combined family.

James stared out the window. "I know my new job as department head has been consuming me—"

You can say that again!

"—but I know Sam better than you do. He went through a difficult patch after Carol died. I think this is a similar thing. Maybe he's just adjusting to you as a new mom. Give him time, and he'll confide in you."

I touched his arm, which was rigid with tension. "Well, okay, that's certainly possible, and I freely admit I don't know Sam as well as you do. But will you talk to him? Just feel him out a little?"

"Lisa, really—"

"I just have this niggling feeling that something's bothering him, something that has nothing to do with this family. A series of events, a relationship, a challenge at school he won't talk about."

James rolled his eyes. "Woman's intuition?"

"If you like." I didn't like; I'd prefer him to think my perception was based on logic and hard evidence. Problem was, I couldn't pin down any hard evidence or remember anything specific. Maybe it was something I'd heard Sam say in the car? Anyhow, now my instinct said it was time to back off the subject. Sweep the problem under the rug...

"Hey, stop frowning or you'll get wrinkles on your forehead." James rumpled my hair.

"I'll just get Botox injections to get rid of them."

"Bad idea."

"Says you."

"Let's go to bed."

"Now, that's a good idea."

Harmony restored, we headed upstairs.

Seven

Friday, January 17

Ellen Perkins entered Charlie's Diner intent upon an infusion of rotgut coffee and a fresh cinnamon roll, dripping with white sugar icing. Maybe the sweetness of the pastry would improve her mood, which was surly and winterish.

Nothing was going right—work sucked, home was only marginally better. And she had weighed in at 141 this morning, two pounds heavier than before. She knew this was a symptom of her life being out of balance, and that knowledge automatically increased both her craving for sugar and fat and her guilt about the craving. A vicious, all-too-familiar circle.

She waited for her order, teetering back and forth on booted feet, thinking about how her passions always got her into trouble. Ellen loved her work, which was artifact conservation, but she was such a perfectionist that minor setbacks—such as the microscope going on the blink or a slip of her scalpel when taking a delicate sample—depressed her.

And then there was Dylan. As her current squeeze, he counted as a passion too, but her heart told her that their relationship was in trouble. It couldn't last. Too many emotional issues between them received short shrift. It seemed that wherever she grew angry with Dylan, they ended up in bed. Bed never solved anything; the sex was usually wonderful, but they didn't really talk things through. And Ellen was experienced enough to know that if her lover was not also her best friend, then the affair was doomed.

What a pity she didn't have a relationship like Lisa and James. James had been her discovery—they'd had a few dates together—but Ellen had to admit she'd never really clicked with James. It was obviously different when he fell in love with Lisa. Lisa had everything now.

Speak of the devil. The door to the diner banged open, and Lisa Donahue blew in on a shower of snow. She smiled at Ellen and joined her at the counter.

"Caffeine injection time?"

"Oh, yeah. Not to mention sugar inhalation." Ellen picked up her order and moved to the nearest table. "Join me?"

"Sure," said Lisa. "Just as soon as I get my coffee."

Ellen shucked off her coat and hiked the chair closer to the tiny round table. Her pang of jealousy died as she observed her old friend leaning against the cash register. Lisa looked tired, and no wonder. It couldn't be easy, stepping up to be Interim Director. None of them had recovered from Victor's brutal demise, but they'd stopped talking about it every day because it was too depressing going over the same speculations with no new facts and no solutions. McEwan and his team had questioned all of them at least three times, but the combined Boston and campus police departments seemed to be making no progress at all.

Lisa plunked down her coffee and pulled out the other chair with a screech of metal legs on the ceramic tiled floor. "How are you today, Ellen?"

Ellen felt a sudden urge to pull back, like a turtle tucking its head inside its shell. She and Lisa usually discussed everything, but Ellen was uncomfortably aware that things had changed since her best friend was now technically her boss. Maybe it wasn't such a great idea to tell Lisa the ins and outs of her affair with another employee. She decided to play it safe and talk about work.

"Disgruntled, I guess," Ellen said. "The conservation work is going so slowly. My student, Eleanor, is very insecure and keeps pestering me with questions. And I have this damn grant to write."

"The one for the Getty Conservation Institute?"

"Yeah."

They talked shop for a while until Lisa changed the subject, venturing into dangerous territory.

"Ellen, have you thought more about who killed Victor?"

They'd had this conversation before, right after it happened. "Of course I have. Just because I don't talk about it doesn't mean I'm not thinking about it. After all, if we have a murderer in the building, we should all be alert to odd behavior."

Lisa's expression hardened. "You know that McEwan thinks it's someone on the museum staff. That means someone with mechanical know-how, someone who could have rigged the cable so it would break—"

Ellen bristled. "If you mean Dylan, it's impossible. He's got no motive!"

"None that you know of," corrected Lisa. "And I didn't mean—"

"Why are you so stuck on Dylan being the criminal? I live with the guy; I'd know if he's been up to no good! Or do you think I'm so infatuated that I wouldn't recognize the signs?"

Lisa closed her eyes.

Ellen threw her napkin over the remains of the cinnamon roll. "Oh, fine! Why don't you just come out and say it, that I'm living with a murderer?"

"I'm not saying anything of the sort!" protested Lisa. "I just want you to keep an open mind."

"There are other candidates, for heaven's sake. Tim Marsden, or George Skirvin—but I don't really think it was him because he's such a nerd—or maybe one of the younger women like Sara Browning—"

"Sara Browning! Now you're really reaching. What's her motive?"

"I've no idea!" Ellen glared at Lisa.

An awkward silence ballooned between them.

"I'm sorry," Lisa said, pushing one hand through the long hair of her pony tail. "This whole thing has been an awful strain on all of us." Her blue eyes pleaded for understanding. "It's just that I've always relied on you to be my sounding board, but now..."

Ellen sighed. "Yeah, now things are different—because you're the boss."

There. She felt calmer now that it was out in the open.

"Yes, I know. But as long as we both recognize that fact, we can still talk." Lisa waited for Ellen's reaction.

Ellen realized Lisa was right. They *could* still talk—just not about everything. She nodded.

"Actually, I did want to ask you what you know about Tim Marsden, particularly about his academic work," Lisa said. "You've known him longer than I have, because you came to the museum first."

"His scholarship? It's okay, as far as I know. Victor said something to me once about how Tim would be outta here, if he'd just stop obsessing over details and write the rest of his dissertation. Apparently, he got hung up by the required literature review in Chapter One because he's one of those people who have trouble completing things. You know, the perennial graduate student who doesn't want to leave the nest. That's why he's been at the university for so long."

"Really? He doesn't look any older than some of the other twenty-somethings."

"He's thirty-four," Ellen said, with a little smile because she knew that would get Lisa. "He did his first M.A. in European history. That took five years; then he switched to art history."

"Good Heavens! I'm only a year older than he is!" Lisa stirred a little more sugar into her coffee. "So, if Victor really didn't recommend him for the Princeton job, as Tim told me, then his decision has nothing to do with how good Tim's thesis is?"

"Right. More likely, it's because Tim has an awkward personality. He's very intense and gets easily irritated by other people's comments. Victor was actually pretty shrewd about which employees would fit well into an academic work environment."

"But Tim isn't any odder than most of the other people who work here."

"True," said Ellen. "We both know this profession attracts everything from nerds to prima donnas. But as far as motive goes, I'd say Tim Marsden hasn't got one. After all, Victor was the head of his committee—and killing off members of his committee sure wouldn't get his thesis approved any faster." She fished out a remnant of the cinnamon roll from under her napkin and popped it in her mouth. "I can see why McEwan thinks the murderer has to be someone on the staff, but so far I can't see that *any* of us has a real motive."

Lisa smiled wearily. "You're right. I've gone round and round, considering all the possibilities, and I'm stumped. It's almost like a malicious ghost dropped that statue on Victor. It's just too hard to connect the crime with a real person." She glanced at her watch. "Yikes, I've got a meeting in ten minutes."

Taking the hint, Ellen stood up and slid her arms into her furry acrylic-lined coat. "Maybe. But try telling that to Sergeant McEwan. I don't think he's quite ready to believe that a ghost cut that cable."

Eight

Wednesday, January 29

C'mon, Lisa, I told myself two weeks later, this job's not so bad. Except for the personnel problems, moving snafus, miscommunication, and tangled finances. Just think about all the new coping skills I'm acquiring.

Today, for example, I was continuing my crash course in building construction in the new Edward G. Taylor Museum.

I stood with the foreman, a hefty forty-something African-American, next to a large puddle on the floor of the foyer leading into the auditorium. "You've told me the roof started leaking after the last snowstorm, but you haven't told me why," I said.

"Well, Dr. Donahue, I don't know why it's leaking. First we have to figure out *where* it's leaking; then maybe we can fix it. I think it's probably around one of the recessed light fixtures over there." He pointed directly overhead.

I looked up, trying to focus on ceiling leaks, but my mind kept returning to earlier that morning. Right after

James had left for work, Sam had refused to eat breakfast and begged to stay home from school.

"Your university engineer is due over here later this morning. Maybe he can tell us." The foreman shrugged.

I smiled ruefully. Both of us knew that the communication between the university Facilities and Management Office, the architect, and the local contractors hadn't been going well. The architect had a huge ego and some peculiar ideas—like cutting off the upper gallery so there'd be a hole in the floor leading from the Asian exhibit to the Americas exhibit directly below. When I'd seen the model, I immediately envisioned fourth graders pitching themselves over the railing. On the other hand, maybe we could allow our Sioux teepee to project upwards—the children wouldn't jump on that.

"Keep me posted, then, Mr. Brown."

He left the room while I stretched cautiously. I'd slept funny and my neck and right shoulder hurt. Classic signs of mental and emotional stress.

Why had Sam wanted to stay home? He wasn't really sick, not really. He hadn't got a temperature, and his only other symptoms were vague stomach pains. What really bothered me was the look of desperation in Sam's eyes.

I continued my casual inspection around the shelled-in auditorium. It would be a beautiful space if they could ever fix the leaky roof. I stood at the top of the stairs, looking down on the mound of packing material heaped up on the stage like one of those plastic ball bins Emma liked so much at "Ants in Their Pants." Briefly I pictured jumping in, making a huge mess as white polystyrene nuggets flew everywhere. Wouldn't that be fitting behavior for my new role as Interim Director?

Instead I left the building and walked back across the Quad, clutching my elderly down parka around my throat. Time for an upgrade—something classy, without a hood. A beige or black wool, full-length coat. Power dressing for a female administrator.

Leaky roof, faulty electricity, budget overruns, and personnel problems. Now I understood why so many of my colleagues hated administration. Instead of spending large blocks of time in library and storeroom preparing for my exhibit, I was spending all my time on the phone or in meetings with the architect and designer. And the Dean was on my case about the new building going over budget.

Thankfully, I entered the overheated atmosphere of Wigglesworth Hall. I debated whether to take the stairs or the elevator, now operational again. Realizing I was unlikely to get any real exercise today, I chose the stairs—the only one of three stairwells that went all the way to the fourth floor. The other two stopped on floors two and three, respectively, prompting frustrated visitors to imitate the "Bert and I" comedians from Maine: "You can't get there from here."

I'd arrived at the fourth floor. Puffing slightly, I viewed the long, dimly lit hallway with fresh eyes. The new facility was slick and modern, but it would never have the character of this building. I crossed to one of the recessed, attic windows that overlooked part of the roof. Numerous openings in the eaves had allowed pigeons to fly in and out of the museum over the years, leaving deposits on our classical and European statues. I smiled as I remembered my first semester when the staff, armed with butterfly nets, chased pigeons out of the galleries on more than one occasion.

Ellen strode into my line of sight. "We've got a problem," she announced. "And maybe you don't want the entire staff to hear about it just yet."

"Let's go to my office," I said, crossing the foyer where our reception desk stood next to a rack of brochures. Ellen's silence as we walked was uncharacteristic—either she was really upset, or she felt the need to distance herself from me as The Boss.

I didn't bother to remove my coat. I flung myself into my swivel chair and took a swig of my cold cappuccino. "Okay, out with it."

"The Bryn Mawr Torque is missing."

I jerked forward and my right shoulder protested with a muscle spasm that traveled down to my wrist.

The Torque was a neck ring, a fourth century B.C. masterpiece of gold, found in Wales. "How the hell did that happen?"

Ellen's normally cheerful face was grim. "I don't know, exactly." She pulled up a chair. "I discovered some of our numbers on the conservation list didn't match the packing roster, so I went to check on the Celtic boxes. When I un-taped the one that was supposed to hold the Torque, I found an empty circular nest in the Ethafoam. I checked a couple more boxes, thinking the first one had been mislabeled, but I can't find it."

I sucked in a long breath. "Have you checked with the other staff? Is there any chance someone else removed the Torque for a legitimate reason?"

"I asked. No one knows anything." Ellen yanked on her short blond hair with one hand as if the pain would help her think. "I don't want to conclude it's a theft, but it's looking more and more likely."

"Then I'll have to tell the Dean—and the police," I said, digging my fingernails into the arm of my chair. "But I'm going to wait until tomorrow, to give you time to double-check."

Ellen fidgeted. "I already have, but I'll do it again," she said shortly.

Oops. She thought I was questioning her competence. "Look, Ellen, I have to ask these questions. I know you're doing everything you can."

Ellen's shoulders relaxed. "The thing is," she said, "we won't know exactly what's missing until we finish unpacking all that stuff in the new building."

Oh, great. We might lose more artifacts during the move. This would take a lot of explaining to Dean Saltonstall. The Bryn Mawr Torque was Victor's prize acquisition for the new European gallery; it had cost the University some eighteen thousand dollars.

I clutched at straws. "Maybe the Torque is still in a box you didn't check?"

Ellen's lip twitched in a parody of a smile. "I don't think so. Remember, Dylan's team is carving out molds in the packing material for each artifact. The Torque won't fit in just any box."

"So it *has* been stolen."

"That's my guess. And probably by someone either on the staff or working with the staff."

"How did you work that out?"

"Access. Who else would know where the valuable stuff was?"

I reached for the phone. "I'll have to tell McEwan now, then. It may be relevant to Victor's death. And then I'll go see the Dean."

Ellen's anxious demeanor dissolved into a sympathetic grin. "I don't envy you, Lisa. Hope Saltonstall doesn't bite your head off."

"I hope so, too. Thanks, Ellen." I punched in the numbers for McEwan's cell phone before I lost my courage.

At least Ellen was still on my side.

~ * ~

Not surprisingly, McEwan was near campus and wanted to see me. I motioned him into my office and shut the door.

As I waited for him to pour himself some dark roast coffee from my French press pot, I wondered why McEwan hadn't been promoted. He seemed so competent; surely in three years he would have been kicked upstairs to the next rank? I decided to ask.

"Sergeant? Weren't you about to become a Lieutenant the last time we met?"

McEwan plunked down his mug and reached for the Splenda and powdered creamer. Without raising his eyes, he said, "Right you are—I was. But in the Boston PD, going up the ladder means less time on the streets and more in front of a computer, filling out goddamn forms. I decided I wasn't ready to be incarcerated just yet." He took a big swig of his doctored coffee and smacked his lips. "Now, tell me the latest."

I described the disappearance of the Torque.

McEwan grunted. "How much is it worth?"

"Purchase price was eighteen thousand. That was three years ago; its worth could easily have increased since then. Ultimately, a piece of art like that is worth whatever someone is willing to pay for it."

"Yeah, and people pay crazy prices for Rembrandts and Picassos—why not fancy Celtic jewelry?"

"And gold can always be recycled," I said dryly. "Melted down and recast as something else. Ancient sculptors did it all the time."

"Great. So Victor was a specialist in Celtic art?"

"Yes."

"So the theft—if it really is a theft—could be related to Victor's murder. Maybe Victor saw or heard something he shouldn't have and that's why he got a statue dropped on him. I'll need to question all the staff members again."

"But the murderer doesn't necessarily have to be someone on the museum staff. It could be someone from another department..." My voice trailed off as I saw McEwan's skeptical expression.

"But another museum employee is the most likely possibility. Do you really believe someone in Sociology is stealing your artifacts?"

"I guess so. I mean, no, it's probably not a sociologist we're looking for. I actually do believe it's someone on our staff, but I don't want to." I gulped, feeling like I'd mangled any meaning in my response. "Actually, there's another possibility."

"What?" McEwan perched on the edge of my desk, waiting.

"So far, you're assuming that who ever took the Torque is the same person who dropped the statue on Victor Fitzgerald. What if someone is stealing artifacts for financial gain, but someone else with a motive we don't know about killed Victor?"

"Huh. A motive like revenge or lust? Sounds like a soap opera. Well, I'll keep that possibility in mind, but I'd certainly prefer one perp instead of two."

I proceeded to pollute the waters even more. "I'm still hoping the Torque will turn up in another box. And that we don't have a thief on the staff."

McEwan sighed. "I can understand why you'd rather not work in a place surrounded by thieves and murderers, but what outsider could possibly know where the valuable artifacts are in the middle of a move? You have boxes upstairs, downstairs, in the hallways..."

He was right, and Ellen thought so, too. No one outside the museum staff could have known which box the Torque was in.

McEwan rubbed his eyes. "Let's go back to Victor's death. Harold Weinberger is out of it. We've checked his whereabouts—he's not even been in town the last few weeks. Now, Miss Blake was dating Victor Fitzgerald, correct?"

"Yes. For about four years now, I think." I spared a thought for Susie, who was still moving around like a zombie. Grief had quenched her normal bubbly enthusiasm.

"What is her background, exactly?" McEwan's pencil hovered over his notebook.

Admiring the way his bushy eyebrows jumped up and down, I said, "Susie's? She used to be a secretary in a law office. But you can't think—you mean, Susie is a suspect? She was in love with Victor!"

McEwan lowered his notebook and pursed his lips. "Everyone is a suspect until proven innocent—remember?"

Even me, though he's pretending I'm an ally.

Out loud, I said," I suppose so.*"*

"Miss Blake seems set on marriage. From what we've found, Victor was avoiding an engagement."

I cocked an eyebrow at him. "A woman like Susie wouldn't kill him because he was indecisive. She'd keep trying to tie him up good and proper."

"Maybe. Unless she knew he was seeing someone else on the sly."

The idea startled me. "Was he?"

"Not that we know of. But I have to consider every possibility. Thanks for the caffeine hit." McEwan nodded and departed to continue his inquiries.

I hauled myself upright and checked my appearance in the pocket mirror on the back of my door. New lines around my mouth greeted me along with pale purple shadows under my eyes. Hmm, I looked like the walking dead. I opened the bottom desk drawer and rummaged in my purse for my compact. I powdered my perennially shiny nose and wished my skin were clearer. How come Ellen's skin always looked perfect, like one of those old-fashioned porcelain dolls?

It was time. I couldn't put off seeing Saltonstall any longer. Feeling like I was on the way to the dentist for a root canal, I clumped down the stairs to the Dean's office on the second floor.

~ * ~

As I trudged home through icy slush mixed with dead leaves, I muttered to myself about my truly awful day.

"Damn McEwan, anyway. He acts like he's playing games with me. One minute, I'm his sidekick. Two seconds later, I'm a bird brain. Then he treats me like a suspect again. Grrr." I squashed a cardboard coffee cup into the sidewalk.

Then there was Dean Saltonstall. "Stuck-up, supercilious prig. If I hear any more about the reputation of the University and his fear of negative publicity, I'll puke."

I had a splitting headache. Naturally. All I wanted now was a long, hot bath and a glass or three of Chardonnay. Alone.

Pure fantasy. Sue, our babysitter, met me at the door with an unwelcome report about Sam.

"He hasn't eaten a thing, Miz Donahue, and I fixed him his favorite melted Swiss cheese with mayo sandwich."

"Nothing at all?"

"Some soda pop—Coke—but that don't count, right?"

"Right. Thanks, Sue."

Sue pulled on her boots and dug out her car keys while I draped my coat over a kitchen chair and kicked off my boots. The wine would have to wait.

I padded down the hall in stocking feet to see Sam. Pausing in the bedroom doorway, I observed the brown-haired little boy propped up with three pillows. He was drawing something complicated on a pad of paper. An almost furless teddy bear perched next to him, observing the project with one beady button eye.

"Hi," I said, approaching the bed.

Sam looked up. "Do we have any big pieces of cardboard? Or poster stuff I could use?"

"Maybe. What are you making?

"A super-Monopoly board. With a real Troll Bridge and a Nudist colony."

I sat on the bed to view the pad he turned towards me. It was actually a double board, one set of squares inside the other. I was amused to see a second "Go," where players could pick up three hundred instead of only two hundred dollars, and a square marked "No Place to Turn Back," decorated with a smoking gun. This was an old Donahue family joke, based on a sign in Maine that was supposed to discourage visitors from visiting a spectacular rocky beach where seals congregated in the spring.

"That looks terrific," I told Sam.

"Thanks. I'm going to get Dad to play it with me when he gets home." Sam showed me the neat stack of Chance and Community Chest cards he was creating to go with the new properties: "The Eiffel Tower," "The John Birch Society," and "Strang's Folly," named after a summer place my father had rented in Maine.

"How's your tummy?" I reached out to touch his pale forehead.

"So-so."

"Think you can go back to school tomorrow?"

Sam's animation disappeared. "Uh—maybe. I dunno. You won't make me if I still feel bad, will you?" he pleaded.

"Not if you're really sick," I said, doing my best to hide my dismay. I stared at the endearing cowlick on the top of his head as he bent over his pad of paper.

Crap, what do I do now? The very mention of school seemed to set him back. I was almost certain that Sam's ulcer-like symptoms were less physical than psychological—and that the root cause had nothing to do with his stepfamily. I resolved to call up the school and talk to Sam's teacher. James would have to listen if the teacher confirmed my suspicions.

I blew my frustration out through my lips.

"Are you okay, Mom?" asked Sam with touching concern.

"Sure. I'm fine. I just want you to get better." I rumpled his hair and trudged out to the kitchen to start dinner.

As I assembled ingredients for what I called "refrigerator-cleaner stir-fry"—leftover meat, veggies, rinds of cheese, and whatever else needed eating quickly. I thought about my husband.

James was so distracted with his new position as a department head that very little of his energy was focused on domestic problems. I loved Sam, but I didn't like the feeling that Sam's well being suddenly rested entirely on my shoulders. Parenting was definitely a two-person proposition. Somehow, I had to carve out more time to talk with James—a time when we weren't exhausted, when the kids were away from home or asleep, when we could explore all the possibilities without interruption.

And what were the odds of finding that time with our hopelessly mismatched schedules?

Nine

Thursday, January 20

It was a gray morning with a raw wind blowing off the Atlantic.

As I pulled in to the museum's parking lot, I noticed a television van.

Oh, hell, reporters.

I gathered up purse and briefcase, calculating how fast I could run through the icy parking lot: not fast enough. And, sure enough, I'd already been spotted.

As I locked my car with one hand while holding my hood on with the other, a young female reporter cornered me and thrust her mike in my face. "Ms. Donahue, right? Tell us what this stolen object is."

Might as well get it over with. "The Bryn Mawr Torque is a type of neck ornament, made of gold, and dating to the fourth-century B.C." I gave as short a statement as I could, steeling myself for the inevitable questions.

"How was the piece stolen from the Museum?"

"We don't know exactly, but it may have been smuggled out in a packing crate along with other artifacts that are being moved to our new building."

"We actually have very little to report at this time," said a smooth baritone voice at my elbow.

Dean Saltonstall. Heat surged under the skin of my neck and face. At his nod, I stepped to one side, allowing the video camera to move to his face.

"The University is making every effort to cooperate with the police," he continued without missing a beat. "All avenues are being explored, and we're sure the artifact will be recovered quickly."

I doubted that. If whoever had snatched it had good connections, the Torque was probably already out of the country. The illegal trade in antiquities was well established, and our little museum was conveniently located near both a major port and a major airport. And Boston was only four hours drive from New York, a city full of dealers and wealthy, private collectors. However, now was not a good time for me to air my inside knowledge of the dark side of archaeology.

I was a little miffed that Saltonstall hadn't allowed me to handle the reporters alone. No doubt he figured that his presence at my side showed institutional solidarity.

Or maybe he thinks a woman won't carry as much credibility with the Press.

Yup, that cynical point of view was probably the correct one, but I could pretend to be charitable. It was, after all, the Dean's job to protect Boston University's image as much as possible. Glancing at his determined profile, I had to admit he was awfully good at it.

Another reporter, this time a tough-looking young man wearing a leather jacket and no gloves, jumped in. "Dean

Saltonstall, what is the connection of this theft with the murder of Victor Fitzgerald, a case that is still unsolved?"

The Dean sighed, his smooth façade splintering. "We don't know if there is a connection, but—"

"And isn't it true that this museum has a history of artifact theft and murder?"

Now I was glad I was no longer on the hot seat—Saltonstall was welcome to it. I listened as the Dean explained that the events of three years ago had nothing to do with Victor's death and the current theft. "Most of the staff has changed since that time period," he finished.

"But you, Ms. Donahue, you were here during the murders three years ago—what do you think?" persisted the reporter.

Catching the grim expression on the Dean's face—this kind of publicity really wasn't good for the University—I said, "I agree with the Dean. There's no connection, and now you'll have to excuse me. I have a meeting in five minutes."

Saltonstall made similar excuses and caught up with me as I entered the building.

"Well, that was about what I expected," I said, as he pushed the "up" button for the elevator and adjusted his tie while we waited for the doors to open.

"Lisa, from what I overheard, you did a good job with those reporters. But how did they find you?"

"They were lurking in the parking lot when I arrived. There was no way to avoid them, and I thought a short statement would mollify them."

"Remember our last conversation? Just say, 'no comment, we'll be sending out a press release later today.'"

"But—"

The Dean stuck one arm in the elevator door to keep it open and turned a stern gaze on me. "Look, you're new at this. I've had a lot of experience with reporters. You know the museum's reputation has been murky ever since your mummy exhibit. I think we need more consistency in how the Press is handled. The next contact you get, refer them to my office."

"Okay, but I understand McEwan is going to talk to reporters later today."

The Dean groaned. "The last time the Boston PD gave a statement, they really made a mess of it! I'll call him right away and see if we can make our stories match."

We rode up to the second floor, where the Dean exited the elevator looking like a thundercloud.

Maybe I didn't play that one so well, I thought uneasily as I continued up to the fourth floor. But he'd be just as critical if I showed no initiative.

I remembered my high school Latin teacher, who was renowned for saying things like, "If you don't learn that declension, I'll have your ears on toast," or even better, "You'll be out in left field without a glove with the sun in your eyes."

Yep, being Director made me feel like an incompetent baseball player.

Ten

Wednesday, February 5

If there's one thing I've learned in this job, it's that nothing ever stays the same—except maybe the artifacts. Vases, lamps, and coins stay in their drawers and cases, collecting dust, while their caretakers vie for power and academic glory.

Less than two weeks after my little media adventure with the Dean, I arrived at work to find a note taped to my monitor: "The Dean wants to see you ASAP."

My stomach dipped. Sudden summonses from Deans were never good news.

Quickly I unwrapped the long green scarf (chenille, and very warm) from around my neck and substituted navy blue flats for my fleece-lined boots. Outside, the snow fell steadily, already blanketing cars in the parking lot below my window and promising a messy commute home. The forecast was dire: six to eight inches, at least. Typical early February in Boston.

"Go right on in, Lisa," said the Dean's secretary when I arrived at the gateway to Deandom.

I walked innocently into Saltonstall's opulently appointed inner sanctum. Instantly, my world turned upside down. I hardly noticed the thick Oriental carpet and the mahogany antique furniture. My attention was riveted on the woman sitting next to the Dean on his VIP couch.

She was dressed to kill in a nifty little black suit with a maroon silk blouse and gold dangly earrings. She sported dark hair, twisted in a low, stylish bun, a beaky nose, and a triumphant expression on her narrow face. It was Valerie Albrecht, my former boss and personal nemesis.

"Hello, David. What did you want to see me about?" I thought I knew what he was about to say, and the very idea made my stomach sink past my shoes into the floor.

He said it. "Lisa—Dr. Donahue—I wanted you to be the first to meet your new Director, Dr. Valerie Albrecht."

Director? Valerie? But I'd just filed my own application for the job! Suddenly I saw flashing lights at the corners of my eyes—clear signs that the migraine I'd been trying to avoid was about to snatch my brain and shred all rational thought.

"Lisa?" asked the Dean, clearly puzzled.

I snapped to attention and stuck out my hand. "Dr. Albrecht," I croaked," Welcome to Boston."

Val's hazel eyes shone with amusement as she gripped my hand with painted talons. "Ms. Donahue," she responded silkily, refusing to acknowledge our identical academic titles. "I'm sure we'll make a fine team."

I gagged. Team! What a joke—Val had no idea what working as a team was about; she preferred dictatorships.

I scarcely heard Saltonstall droning on because my mind was churning with memories of the museum in Philadelphia. All-nighters because Val couldn't decide until the last minute what she wanted on display. Exhibit labels written within forty-eight frantic hours and the writers subjected to arbitrary and impossible standards. Memos lost in the black hole of Val's office. Public dressings-down of staff members—naturally, nothing was ever Val's fault—that demoralized everyone.

"She has a distinguished background working in museums in Germany before she came to the U.S. I'm sure her scholarship will boost the profile of our little museum, and the faculty will respond favorably to her exhibit plans."

Never mind that her staff would fall like ninepins. Working for Val was like lying injured and helpless in a meadow while vultures hovered overhead.

"Why don't you tell Lisa some of your ideas, the ones we discussed in New York?"

Val smiled. "Of course, Dave, I'd be delighted to."

Dave? Since when was the proper and stuffy Saltonstall called "Dave?"

".Lisa, I'm sure you remember some of the changes I made in Philadelphia..."

Boy, did I ever.

"...every gallery will be revamped before the new building opens... new educational programming... all the latest museology..."

I nodded and murmured in appropriate places and fought the pounding of the fully realized migraine inside my head.

"David—Dean..." I floundered over what to call him now that I'd been demoted, and Val's eyes gleamed. "Do you want me to tell the rest of the staff about this appointment?"

"No, Lisa," said Val in a smarmy tone. "I'll do that—after Dave and I have lunch."

I was not invited.

"Dave" Saltonstall helped Val on with her possum fur coat. No doubt he'd take her to a nice restaurant like Luigi's or Locke-Ober using taxpayer dollars. "Valerie," he said unctuously, "we have to hustle. Sergeant McEwan's coming at one-thirty to bring you up to date on our recent crime wave."

I turned away from Val's malicious little smile and staggered toward my office. Behind me, I could hear the clack-clack of Val's heels beating on the polished floor.

Soon those heels would be pecking at my ego, bit by bit, until all that remained was an eyeless shadow of my former self.

~ * ~

"No... ooo!" Ellen's reaction was a predictable yell of outrage. "I left Philly to get away from that woman!" She slammed her mug on the ancient coffee table and paced the rejected classroom that served as our staff lounge, her blonde bob bouncing with the force of her fury.

I winced. I'd taken some Ibuprofen for my migraine, but it was too soon for it to do any good, and Ellen's shriek penetrated my tender brain like a knife cutting soft cheese.

"I know. So did I. I can't stand the thought of being around her again. Maybe I should get out my old bottle of

Prozac." Even Prozac wouldn't stop the churning of stomach acid that Val's very presence caused in me.

"And I should get my doctor to write me a prescription. How on earth did she get decent references after Philadelphia?"

Our lovely but sneaky boss had been suspected of embezzling, but nothing was ever proven against her. Val was too good at bending rules while the higher ups were looking the wrong way.

"Maybe someone lied to get rid of her. Or she smarmed all over someone with connections. University administrators don't care that she's hell on her staff as long as she sucks up to the Right People and brings in the big bucks," I said.

"How the hell did she get hired so fast?"

"Dean Saltonstall must have cut corners on this one. It's less than a month since Victor died. Must have advertised online." A memory surfaced. "And he said something about meeting her in New York."

"Maybe she seduced him. Whatever. This is a catastrophe for us! Maybe we could drop another statue on her." Ellen flung herself into the shabby orange armchair, a Salvation Army relic that cluttered up our staff lounge.

That idea certainly appealed to me. "If you can figure out a way to do it without getting caught, let me know." I pressed my thumbs into the corners of my eye sockets, searching for the acupressure points that would relieve my headache. Try the temples, harder now...

"Hey, wait a minute!" cried Ellen, leaning forward. "Didn't you just apply for the Director's job?"

"Yeah." Delayed anger surged in my veins. Good old Saltonstall had bypassed me completely. "Guess the Dean—Val calls him 'Dave'—wanted someone from off-campus—or else he didn't like the idea of promoting from inside the museum staff."

"You mean, because you've been on the staff already, you might not exert the necessary authority?"

"Something like that," I said, wondering if I really could make that permanent transition from employee to employer with any credibility or grace.

Ellen jumped up and paced the narrow space between couch and fridge. "I'd rather have you any day over Val. But maybe it's better this way."

"How could it be better with Val in charge?"

"You and I—and everyone else on the staff—will be more united than we've ever been before. Against her."

I snorted. "Small comfort." But then I remembered the uneasy vibes I'd received from the other staff while I'd been Interim Director. "You could be right."

Eleven

Monday, February 10

Ellen watched as Valerie Albrecht smoothed her hair and straightened her slender, stocking-clad legs under the table. "Now that we've all introduced ourselves," she said, "I'm going to tell you about the changes I'll be making." Val stacked the papers in front of her neatly and smiled, showing all her teeth.

Just like a man-eating tiger, thought Ellen as she observed how her new boss took in the fidgeting of the younger staff. Someone coughed and a chair leg scraped the floor. Tensions seethed and swirled around her as everyone waited for Val's next move.

Ellen tried to put herself in Val's shoes. What was the old witch thinking as she looked around the room?

Probably Val was amused to have Lisa and Ellen under her thumb again. And, no doubt, she was thrilled to have new staff to break in. She'd do that with a combination of sweet-talking and impossible demands—what Ellen's mom called a set-up for failure. Butter up one of the younger women so that she thought she was worthy of her new responsibilities, then give her an assignment she couldn't possible complete.

Lisa looked pale and her shoulders drooped. She'd always been thin-skinned, and from what Ellen had seen, Lisa hadn't been Director long enough to grow a proper suit of emotional armor. And she'd reacted to the Dean's perfidy in passing her over with depression rather than anger—a bad sign in Ellen's book.

"One change I'm making is in public relations," Val said. "I have more experience than any of you in that area, so all press releases and media contacts will go through my office, not through Susie Blake as in the past. We want to present the best possible image to the rest of the University and the outside world. Understood?"

Ellen saw how Susie stiffened in her chair. Everyone else nodded, their eyes avoiding each other.

"Also, I will be keeping different hours than Victor did since I'm doing some additional fundraising work for the Dean. I'll be in ten to three, except Fridays, when I will work from home."

Ten to three! So Val thought she could rule with an iron hand while she kept banker's hours! Ridiculous!

"Nancy here will keep track of my schedule." Val nodded at Nancy Phelan, whose brown eyes widened as she bobbed her head.

Oh, right. Nancy was an apple-polisher and a doormat. Her pliant nature and eager-beaver attitude would appeal to Val much more than Susie's take-charge manner and seasoned professionalism.

As Val continued to itemize her changes, Ellen watched Susie. Susie's posture was rigid and her eyes glittered like blue ice. She was used to being the boss's eyes and ears; she wouldn't take kindly to being demoted—and she was much better at expressing anger than Lisa.

Val's voice thickened until it sounded almost like a purr. "Now let's have your reports. Dylan? You first." She crossed her elegant legs and leaned back in her chair. Dylan adjusted his shoulders to a more flattering angle and spoke with just the right amount of deference. As he summarized the packing and moving data, he smoothed his hair with one well-manicured hand. Val's gaze roved over his muscled arms and her lips curved ever so slightly.

Oh, brother. Ellen's stomach churned. She could read the signals as well as anyone. Val was interested in Dylan, and he was responding! She couldn't tell whether he was just playing up to her—he was a dreadful flirt, after all—or whether he was really attracted to her. Ellen had heard enough about Dylan's previous relationships to realize that his experience was even broader than her own. And that it included married women. She'd been kidding herself when she'd thought that Dylan had changed. He had a very peculiar moral code, and the fact that a woman he was attracted to was also his boss would not deter him.

A hard lump of anger nearly choked her. She pictured two heavy statues poised over the heads of Val and Dylan. She'd wait until just the right moment and release the cables.

Ellen shoved her chair forward so the arms slammed against the conference table. Everyone jumped. Val kept her cool, but Dylan looked suddenly deflated.

"Sorry," Ellen said sweetly.

But not as sorry as you're gonna be, Valerie Albrecht.

~ * ~

"Well, Lisa, you've been Interim Director for how long now, a month?"

I settled myself on the other side of the small table in my former office and regarded my new boss warily. "About that, yes."

"Long enough to make some contacts and sort out some problems. Tell me every single thing you have done, every person you've talked with—especially about the new building."

I complied, and felt her laser beam eyes probing my brain. I deliberately held back my character assessments of people and kept my account dry and factual. "...The chief architect for the new building is Carl Abrams, and his assistant is Dick Bielaski."

Val homed in on the missing information. "Is Carl easy to work with?"

Carl was a slimy bastard who hated dealing with women. "Ah—he's a bit difficult, but he responds to flattery."

"You don't like him, do you?" Her smile implied that I was therefore too much of a sissy to deal with him.

"Not particularly, but I've had no problems communicating with him." I relaxed my hands, which had begun to clench into fists, and froze my face into a bland mask.

"Hmm." Val glanced over her notes and then said, without looking up, "Now, I want all your files on the building progress and any dealings with the other staff members so I can get up to speed quickly."

Sure thing, you bitch.

I opened my briefcase, feeling smug at my foresight in making copies before this meeting. With a little flourish, I handed Val a sheaf of neatly labeled folders.

Val's eyebrows rose.

So she'd expected a little protest, a little non-compliance from me! Maybe she didn't think I was a complete doormat after all.

"I assume all this stuff is backed up on the computer in this office?" said Val.

I nodded. I didn't add that everything was also backed up on my own laptop and the memory stick I carried back and forth to work. Val's short hours at the museum meant she was going to be very busy—busier than she imagined—and I intended to remain fully prepared to attend the architectural meetings. Val had already announced she wanted to interview all the staff and revamp their job descriptions, so like it or not, she'd have to assign some of the other responsibilities to me. Of course, if anything went wrong during the building negotiations, then Val would have someone—me—ready to take the fall.

Oh yes, I was thoroughly familiar with Val's operating style.

"And by the way," Val said with a little gleam in her brown eyes.

"Yes?" I said, wondering what was coming now.

"You're no longer a member of the police investigation team. Dean Saltonstall told Sergeant McEwan to report directly to me about his progress. We agreed that's only proper, since I wasn't even in Boston when Victor was killed. After all, the rest of you are all possible suspects until proven innocent."

"Actually, we're 'innocent until proven guilty,' Val," I snapped.

She just smiled.

How typical, I thought as I left her office. Val wants to make me squirm by reminding me that I'm still a suspect.

Would McEwan obey the Dean in this matter and leave me out of the loop? He could be quite stubborn about doing things his own way. Time would tell, but I had the uneasy feeling that I was now an outsider—in every way.

Twelve

Wednesday, February 12

James Barber began the day in a surly mood. Trying to be helpful, he'd offered to take the kids to school to give Lisa more time to get ready. But of course, he'd chosen a day when traffic was backed up on Boylston St. Frustrated at running late, he'd forgotten Sam's lunch box. Then he'd driven a whole block with the emergency brake on, which wasn't good for his aging VW bug.

As he locked his car in the garage under Beth Israel Deaconess Hospital near Fenway Park, he thought about the change in his wife since the reappearance of Valerie Albrecht. Normally, Lisa projected confidence and competence. She was, after all, an experienced museum curator who had done well in her Boston job. But Val seemed to have a destabilizing effect on most of her employees.

He climbed the five flights of stairs to his office rather than taking the elevator, cataloguing Lisa's symptoms: restlessness, nightmares, grumpiness with the children, and no interest in sex. James was a patient man, but he wished fleetingly that stress would make Lisa more eager for intimacy rather than less. Maybe if he lit some candles, gave her a good backrub, bought her bittersweet chocolate...

"Hey, Barber," said his colleague David Caldwell. "Charlie Sloan called about some urgent X-rays he wants you to look at. He said he'd be in the morgue until eleven, and then in his office if you need him."

"Right, thanks," James said, draping his Land's End jacket over his chair and rolling up his sleeves.

He sniffed the aroma of fresh Java and wandered over to the coffee pot. Damn, it was empty—David and Marcie had already slurped up the first one. Why couldn't the folks who emptied the pot start a new one? Irritably, he opened his private stash of Starbuck's French Roast and poured water through the filter.

James booted up the "Virtual Man" program and opened his inbox, scrolling down until he found the digital files from Charlie. After a few minutes of studying them, he understood why they'd been marked "urgent." The body showed fractures in the occipital area of the skull and along the collarbone. Beaten with a blunt instrument? Must be a forensic case.

He took the stairs again—good for clearing the brain as well as stretching the leg muscles—- holding the big envelope easily under one arm. What would he carry around with him when Radiology went completely digital in another few months? A laptop or a tablet PC, he supposed—anything smaller would be useless for reading X-rays efficiently.

As James approached the morgue, an odd, shrill muttering caught his attention.

"The face flap is connected to the forehead, the chest wall is anchored by the muscle..."

Sounded like that old song, "de hip bone is connected to de thigh bone..." Who was singing?

"Now we take out the organs, brain-intestines-liver-lungs-stomach...Okay! Now we got a cavity. Let's add the salts and dry it all out, yessir..."

Sounded like the first steps for making an Egyptian mummy. How bizarre.

"Then we make it stink pretty, add lots of aromatics... who you gonna wrap, now? What you gonna wrap with? Pull out the household linens!"

James tiptoed up to the door and peeked inside. The *diener*, Steven Trendall, was doing a slow shuffle dance around the autopsy table, waving a knife in the air as he chanted his recipe.

Whew. Was this guy abnormal, or did he just have a weird sense of humor, like most pathologists?

"Getting ready for your next patient?" asked James, stepping inside the morgue.

Steven, not missing a step, spun gracefully around and laid the knife on the counter with a tiny clink. "Oh, hi, Dr. Barber," he said in a completely normal voice. "Yeah, we've got an old gomer to autopsy—eighty-five if he's a day."

James noticed a small Egyptian tattoo—a miniature Osiris?—on Trendall's right arm. He decided to play along, and see what transpired. "Ah, well someone that old is already half desiccated, right?" He'd said the right thing; the *diener's* eyes brightened.

"Not as much as you'd think," said Steven, leaning back against the sink. "If it's someone who was poorly looked after the last week or two of life and got dehydrated, maybe a bit. But, see, the guts have to come out and be separately treated before the chest cavity can really dry out..." He licked his lips.

James owed his intimate knowledge of mummies to Lisa. He remembered Lisa's silly mnemonic for the organs that caused decay. "Intestines, Liver, Lungs, and Stomach: ILLS," he intoned.

"'ILLS', I like that," Steven cackled. "So you're into mummies, too?"

"My wife is. She's an archaeologist, and her museum did a mummy project about three years ago at BU."

"Oh, that one! Saw the web page, so cool. We should mummify everyone the way the Egyptians did..." He babbled on while he wiped down the table with bleach, talking about how to find the best salts for the desiccation process and the best pine resins for preserving the skin. "They used honey for preservation too, and bitumen from the Dead Sea."

"Where do you get all this information?" James asked.

Steven looked surprised. "Online, man. And from a few great books. There's one by this pathologist in Minnesota, Arthur Aufderheide. His book, *The Scientific Study of Mummies*, is just awesome. It's about mummies from all over the world. Not just Egyptian ones, but mummies from the Canary Islands and Chile and Peru. And there are websites packed with information. Wanna see?" He moved the bleach container over to the sink and headed for the alcove that docs and *dieners* used to change. A small terminal had been set up next to the lockers.

James followed Steven, curious about the obvious passion in the guy's voice. He also wondered if there were new websites since Lisa had completed her research.

Steven stripped off his gloves, closed the patient record program (working without a hitch, for a change), and opened the Firefox browser. He moved the cursor to Bookmarks and quickly scrolled down a long list of mummy-related sites.

James reflected ruefully that here was a dandy example of employees using the hospital computer to surf the Internet when they were supposed to be working. Well, at least it wasn't pornography.

"Look at this one," said Steven, with a distinct note of glee in his voice.

The website was labeled "How to Make Your Own Mummy," and had fascinating graphics of dead moles, rabbits, and frogs in various stages of preservation. James leaned over Steven's shoulder as he opened various links.

"See, Dr. Barber, you can even find recipes for different ways to embalm animals. Here's one using juniper berries, honey, and red wine vinegar. Or you can just bury a body in honey. Herodotus says that's what the ancient Babylonians did."

James frowned. "Why would honey work?"

"Uh—something about osmosis of the sugars. Honey has some anti-microbial properties, too."

Hmm, thought James. Weird and interesting stuff.

Dieners tended to be odd—you had to be little odd to tolerate being an autopsy assistant and working in a morgue. Trendall seemed smart enough; he'd clearly absorbed a certain amount of book learning about the more esoteric aspects of embalming and mummy-making from different cultures and parts of the world. And Charlie and Mic obviously thought his work was okay—at least Mic had no complaints.

"Well, if you see Charlie, tell him I stopped by. He knows where to find me," said James.

"Sure thing," Steven said. He closed Firefox and opened a handy drawer near the lockers for new surgical gloves.

As James took the stairs two at a time, he reflected that people who had a passion, no matter how weird, possessed a better work ethic than those who didn't. He was terribly afraid his own passion for clinical medicine was waning; he kept having daydreams about taking an academic post where he could do the kind of research that Lisa did—when she wasn't playing administrator. What would it be like to bury yourself in the library for hours at a stretch, chasing down interesting references until you knew everything you wanted to about a subject? He hadn't had that kind of experience in years—the workload at Beth Israel was so great that James, like all his colleagues, had learned the fine art of skimming. No one had time to dwell on details; everyone skimmed through charts and reports, searching for nuggets of hard information and shoving the rest aside.

Back in his office, James decided to allow himself fifteen minutes of web surfing. Just for the hell of it, what kind of jobs were out there, right now? He pictured answering an ad that read, "One ivory tower for rent: low-stress research job for true scholar. Fully-equipped, state-of-the-art office and luxury apartment, no committee work."

Dream on, James. He wasn't kidding himself about the nature of medical academics—the blissful hours in the library would be offset by long hours teaching basic courses and a whole new set of administrative garbage.

But an ivory tower, even a mildewed and antiquated one, would make a nice change.

Thirteen

Friday, February 14

Finally, it was the weekend.

It had been a killer week for both of them. James and Lisa left Sam and Emma with a babysitter and walked over to Dylan and Ellen's apartment for dinner to celebrate Valentine's Day.

James, feeling distinctly out of sorts, zipped his Land's End parka up all the way against the bitter wind and pulled down the earflaps on his hat. He was exhausted; a movie at home would have been more his speed tonight. Trying for an upbeat tone as they turned the corner, he said, "Hey, Lisa, there's a guy in our morgue who's interested in mummies."

"Really? Is he a pathologist?"

"No, a *diener*." He told her about his conversation with Steven.

"Aufderheide's book, huh? Guy has good taste. That's one of my favorite books."

"He's a bit odd, though," James said. "Kinda fixated on his subject."

Lisa laughed. "You say that? Normally I'd say that's odd, but I suppose Egyptian embalming is a natural sideline for someone who works with dead bodies all day."

"Yeah. One corpse is very much like another." He said this with a smile, knowing how Lisa would respond.

She hit him lightly on the arm with her mittened hand. "That's just another way of saying 'all cats are alike in the dark,' isn't it?"

Lisa had once asked him if his ob-gyn rotation had changed his attitude about female bodies. He'd replied that on one level, everyone was the same: the human body was a machine with parts, almost like an automobile. Sometimes parts needed repair or adjustment.

"But if you love a woman, it's different—isn't it?"

"Of course. But you can't ignore the fact that some bodies are more attractive than others. And the sex act is basically the same, no matter who you're doing it with."

Lisa had conceded that on a mechanical level, that was true, but it sure wasn't romantic.

Now, as they climbed the steps to Dylan's apartment building, she glanced at James and said, "Speaking of cats, there may be some fur flying tonight."

"Oh? Ellen and Dylan have a fight?"

"Not exactly. Dylan is flirting with our new boss, and Ellen said—"

Lisa left her sentence unfinished as their host opened the door.

"Hello, Lisa! James, it's great to finally meet you. Come right on in!"

James shook hands with Dylan, observed his sleek dark hair and buff physique, and took an instant dislike to him.

"I smell garlic," Lisa said as she shucked off her black down coat and mittens.

Ellen poked her head out of the kitchen. "And onion, and artichokes, and tomatoes..."

"And black olives and capers and mushrooms. It's a great new sauce I got out of that Mediterranean cookbook," Dylan said.

Oh, spiffy. Another guy who thought he was God's gift to cooking—and that he therefore had an inside track with women. James had met the type before and distrusted any man who was more at home in the kitchen than in the garage or woodshop.

Ellen handed him an open Sam Adams beer bottle, and they exchanged a private smile.

"How are you, Ellen?" James, who had briefly dated Ellen before he met Lisa, thought she was looking well except for tiny lines of strain around her eyes. This was unusual; Ellen's face normally radiated enthusiasm and optimism. James concluded that Dylan was responsible for those fine lines.

"I've been better," Ellen admitted. "I assume Lisa's told you about the return of the Dragon Lady? Losing Victor that way was upsetting enough; having Val back in our lives ranks at least ninety degrees on the Stressometer."

James grinned at the reference to the now famous Stressometer. He sipped his beer and wondered how long it would take Ellen to figure out that Dylan was bad news, a "Toxic Man in Your Life." Seeing her goofy smile and the way she touched Dylan's arm as he stirred the pot, James decided Ellen was still too enamored to recognize his true nature.

"Val's not so bad," Dylan said unwisely. He missed the narrowing of the eyes of both females present and ignored Ellen's dropping the bread knife on the floor. "She's really savvy about fund-raising and handling the media. She'll bring in new blood for the Board. And when I told her I was thinking about getting another degree, she was full of suggestions."

Way to go, Luneau, don't pay any attention to the reactions of people around you. James turned his gaze from Dylan's smug face to Lisa's somber one, observing the slightly pinched skin around her mouth. Lisa disliked Dylan, partly because he was a difficult colleague, but especially because of his effect on Ellen. James was pretty sure Lisa wouldn't have accepted the dinner invitation unless she felt her best friend needed moral support. His mission tonight was to help Lisa pretend everything was normal; they were just two friendly couples having dinner together.

"Val's great at public relations," Lisa said, pouring herself more Chardonnay. "But she's hell on people who work under her. She's smooth and she's plausible. You start out feeling that Val is interested in you and your future and then, wham! She's figured out your vulnerabilities and is using them against you."

"Yeah," Ellen said, leaning against the island as she took an olive from the antipasto platter. "Oh, this one's yummy; it's stuffed with goat cheese." She swallowed a bite. "You're sitting pretty, thinking maybe your museum career is finally launched, and then the floor caves in under you."

"Whew! I find that hard to believe," Dylan said as he reached for his newest stainless steel gadget: the pepper grinder to end all pepper grinders. It looked like a turret for a castle. "You know, some powerful women find other women threatening—maybe she doesn't know how to work with other females with advanced degrees." His dark brown eyes glistened with sincerity.

Ellen grunted and exchanged a meaningful glance with Lisa as she moved around the table laying silver and cloth napkins.

"Good theory, Dylan," said James. "But I know from Lisa's stories about the museum in Philadelphia that Val's been hell on a couple of guys, too. She seems to be a kind of human steamroller—everyone in her path gets flattened."

Dylan raised one dark eyebrow. "Oh, really? Well, she won't flatten me."

James saw Lisa's mouth thin to a determined line and smiled.

Ah, but you deserve to be flattened. Maybe my clever wife will do it.

Out loud he said, "Hey, is that pasta ready yet? I'm starving."

Fourteen

Monday, February 17

The following week, the weather broke enough for Ellen and Susie to consider walking to the Golden Buddha for lunch. They sidestepped puddles as they crossed Commonwealth Ave. and turned onto Sheraton.

Susie pushed the door open, releasing the heavenly aroma of steamed pork, anise, and ginger.

"That woman is the living end. I can't understand how she pulled the wool over the Dean's eyes." Susie said. She hadn't stopped talking about their new boss since they'd left the museum.

Ellen found a table near the wall and shucked off her coat and gloves over the extra chair.

As they waited for the dim sum cart to reach their table, Ellen realized that Susie Blake had joined the ranks of staff members who wanted something large and heavy to squash Valerie Albrecht, the sooner the better.

Not that Ellen blamed her. As far as she was concerned, Val deserved to be pinned like a poisonous beetle to a card—then dried out, catalogued, and stuffed in a glass-topped drawer. Ellen smiled at the mental image and watched Susie, who was on the verge of throwing won tons.

Susie ignored the people around her in the Chinese restaurant and glared at her chopsticks. "I'm the Assistant Director and Val has just left me hanging! I've suddenly got no duties, except for filing, because she's given them all to that simpering Nancy."

The long-awaited cart full of tempting, dough-wrapped surprises arrived and they made their selections.

"It's a new Director's prerogative to change staff assignments," Ellen said as she speared her first dim sum with a chopstick. "You know that, Susie. Just make yourself indispensable and she'll realize your worth." She bit into a fragrant package with pork, chilies, and green onion, savoring the delicate contrast of flavors. She might as well eat her own words; she remembered all too well the shake-ups Val had caused in staff jobs at the Philadelphia museum five years ago.

"It's not that simple." Susie tossed her hair and locked her gaze onto Ellen's face. "I get the feeling she's enjoying baiting me, waiting for me to crawl up and beg for my old position. Then she can have the pleasure of turning me down, saying I'm better suited to word-processing or paying invoices."

Ellen had always known that Susie was sharper than her red curls and lush figure led people to expect. "You're probably right. Valerie Albrecht likes to play with a person like a cat with a small bird. Push her around, then sit back and let her think the danger's over, then squash her with a velvet paw. She does it just for fun."

"Oh, come off it! You're getting as bad as Lisa with all your cat allusions. And I am not a bird, or a mouse, to be batted around."

"Yeah. Well, I see a lot of Lisa's cat, and he's a killer." Ellen smiled as she remembered how Oreo "killed" his indoor toys at the Donahue-Barber apartment. The cat's current favorite was a mangy scrap of rabbit fur tied to a bit of rawhide that was due to disintegrate any time now. "Besides, Lisa told me that cats were sacred in ancient Egypt. That justifies talking about them all the time."

"I hate cats," Susie said, shoving aside her plate. Her baby blue eyes darkened to lapis lazuli. "I am not a glorified secretary. The very next time Val asks for a grant file, I'll show her how hard it is to operate without me."

"Don't push it too far. Val is just itching to fire someone." Ellen reached for the brown ceramic teapot and poured them both more jasmine tea.

Susie drew herself up to what would be her full, statuesque five feet, eight inches tall if she weren't sitting down. "I'm a permanent employee with excellent reviews. She can't fire me." Her voice was loud enough to cause several other diners to turn their way.

Ellen reached out and grasped Susie's wrist. "Believe me, Susie. Val doesn't play by the rules. She does as she pleases, and she usually gets away with it. She fired five 'permanent' employees in Philadelphia before the ink was dry on her own appointment."

"Yeah, well, she's got to learn I'm no doormat like Nancy."

Doormat? Susie? Ellen bit back a laugh. Susie was as a house cat lying on its back with twenty claws at the ready.

There. She'd done it again. Susie was right—Ellen was using too many cat allusions. She'd have to switch to guinea pigs or something. Or little white rats? That fit their situation better anyhow: rats shivering on an icy deck while Valerie, the Queen of Rats, headed their ship straight for a giant iceberg.

What a depressing image. Ellen shivered and used her chopstick to spear another dim sum.

~ * ~

"Now, Lisa, you know we can't have labels this long." Valerie skimmed the label copy, making huge red X's through text I'd slaved over for weeks. "And you can't put in this much technical detail. Remember, you're writing for the general public."

I gnashed my teeth and thought about ripping out hunks of hair—hers, not mine. "General public" to Val meant a third-grade reading level at best. I'd been writing exhibit copy for years, usually without this kind of micromanaging. What made it worse was that Val "edited" materials just before crucial deadlines, making it impossible to finish the massive corrections without a last minute panic.

"I have done this before," I said lamely, shifting my weight on the hard, straight-backed chair Valerie kept for visitors to her office. Naturally, she'd replaced the comfortable upholstered armchair used by Victor. My intestines knotted as I realized what Val was going to do—destroy my carefully laid plans for staying on top of the exhibit by insisting on major changes.

Valerie looked up from the sheaf of paper, her hazel eyes reflecting malicious amusement. "Of course you have, Lisa, but while I'm here, we'll do things my way. I have much more experience in the museum business than you do. When I was in Berlin..."

Oh, crap. I'd heard all the Berlin stories before and had no desire to hear them again. I did my best not to fidget. Val just *loved* the opportunity to educate younger staff.

"In Germany, you see, the standards are much higher. No text is ever put up on the wall without the most stringent review. I'm doing you a favor, Lisa, in making you get it right the first time." Val's voice droned on and became even more condescending.

Get it right the first time? Depends on what you mean by "right." I bet nine-tenths of the museum visitors would appreciate my writing style—they had before—but it was no good saying this to Valerie. It made no difference to her that our institution was a university museum with a largely over-educated clientele. She only understood the Disney approach to museum programming.

"Lisa, pay attention! I don't like the title of this exhibit. 'Earth and Fire: The Ceramic Industry in the Ancient Mediterranean.' Sounds much too academic." She thought for a moment. " 'Potting for Posterity: Masterpieces of Greek and Roman Art.' Use that."

My hands grew clammy. Breathing through my nose and digging my fingernails into my clipboard, I spoke with commendable restraint. "But this isn't an art exhibit, it's an anthropology exhibit! No, the themes we agreed upon were technology and trade patterns—the way the Greeks and Romans used slave labor for the actual production and set up satellite factories all over—"

"That was what you agreed on with Victor, not me."

I stared at her smug expression. "But I've been working on selecting artifacts and composing appropriate text for this exhibit for months!"

"You forget; I did one of my doctoral exams in Greek vase-painting, just as you did. And we have some rather choice vases here. You need to rework the labels in the Greek section; include some of the iconography. The technology is only part of the story."

"But it will look funny if we change the exhibit name at this late date. The publicity has already gone out—"

"No, it hasn't. I held back your press release until after this meeting."

Stupid, interfering bitch. So now the flyers announcing the exhibit would be late!

Val dropped the heavily marked copy back into my lap and stood up. "Better get back to work, Lisa, if you're going to make your deadline."

I seized my papers and resisted the intense desire to ram them down Val's scrawny throat. "I'll do my best," I said, "but because there's so little time, I may have to take a few shortcuts. In fact, I don't think Printing Services can turn over copy this fast. If we did it in house, on our newest Power Mac..."

"We've been over that! I won't compromise on printing standards just because you're slow to produce what I want! Do it right, and make sure all my corrections are included," Val said, her hawk-like gaze holding mine. "Why, you've got five whole days before the Opening!" She waltzed away towards the Conservation lab, no doubt to spike Ellen's guns next.

My legs trembled with the force of my anger and dismay. I shuffled toward my office. Halfway there, I reversed course and headed for the staff lounge. I needed coffee, strong coffee, before I could deal with this debacle.

Fifteen

Same day, afternoon

Ellen, exiting the third floor workshop with a diet Coke, saw Val bustling away from her down the hall and guessed that the Boss from Hell was headed toward the Conservation Lab. Stepping back into the doorway so Val wouldn't spot her if she turned around, Ellen thought about her best strategy for avoiding trouble.

No doubt Val wanted to interrogate Ellen about conservation methods. She, Ellen, wasn't about to let that happen until she'd finished writing out her procedures to her own satisfaction. Ellen knew her boss was systematically going through the staff, forcing each person to define her job and then justify every single thing she did. Besides teaching Val the inner workings of her new kingdom, this approach gave her the chance to tinker with each job description so that the employee had no doubt at all about who was in charge.

Ellen's lower lip curled as she saw Val touch her elegant French braid, pausing to gaze at her reflection in the glass window of the Sociology Department's main office. Val liked to look good, and she was fully aware that wearing designer suits and Italian shoes exuded power and success to her female staff. No one, except for Susie, could compete in that department—another reason why Val wanted to put Susie in the shade.

A screech of metal wheels caught Ellen's attention and she looked past Val.

Uh oh—here comes "Georgie-Porgie."

George Skirvin, pushing a cart full of artifacts, turned the corner into Val's path. Ellen tensed, sure of a confrontation ahead. George, with his acne-ridden skin and his baggy clothes that always looked slept in, was bound to irritate Val. She wouldn't approve of his sullen attitude or whiny voice, either.

Delicate and expensive ancient Greek vases crammed both the upper and lower shelves of George's cart. George reached the elevator and pushed the "down" button. Oblivious to Val's presence, he leaned against the wall and stared vacantly at the floor while his headphones pulsed music into his overlarge ears. His left foot pushed the cart away from him. George reached out to grab it, but missed. Instead, his clumsy fingers tipped a tall *oinochoe*, a black-figured pitcher, over the edge. Val lunged for the cart just as the vase hit the floor and smashed into a trillion pieces.

Valerie grabbed the startled George by the arm. Her voice rose in outrage. "Who taught you to move valuable Greek vases that way? Don't you know the first thing about bracing objects with sandbags when they're in motion?"

"Yes, Dr. Albrecht. I do know how to do that, but Dr. Donahue wanted them quickly, and I thought..."

"Clearly, you didn't think! This is the second incident of this nature since I arrived, and that's two too many. You're fired; you can clear out your desk immediately. I don't want to see your fat face around here again."

George hunched his shoulders and sniveled. "Dr. Albrecht, please give me another chance—I really need this job. You see, Dr. Fitzgerald promised..."

"What Victor promised or didn't promise is irrelevant to me. You're out, and you will stay out. Leave the cart there; I'll get Dylan to see to it." Val pushed the elevator button viciously.

Ellen gasped as George kicked a large potsherd halfway down the hall. Then, his shoulders sagging, he turned his back on both of them and slouched towards the stairs.

As her gaze shifted, Ellen discovered Val had turned and was looking straight at her.

Ooops.

"There you are, Ellen. Time for a chat. Let's go into your lab."

Cursing under her breath, Ellen followed Val back to the elevator.

~ * ~

Back in my office, I sweated over my labels, squinting at Val's horrible cursive handwriting scrawled over the sheets of paper. Why couldn't the witch learn to print?

I'd figured out how to incorporate the iconography Val wanted in the exhibit without scrapping the huge amount of text I'd already written. By moving just five artifacts to another part of the display, I gained most of a case to deal with themes in Greek vase painting, with a header label "From Battle to Boudoir." Five new vases showed scenes of warriors, athletes, weavers, and women bathing and adorning themselves with jewels—all the different aspects of Greek daily life.

I mulled over the wording of a section on "The Sports Illustrated of the Ancient World." I wanted a sidebar describing how the curved surfaces of Attic black and red figured pitchers and *kraters* (wine-bowls) were the best visual records of the first Olympic Games since most monumental wall painting had not survived.

Then, for balance, I would add a small panel on the iconography of stamped Roman lamps and bowls, especially those with mythological scenes. We had a nifty little bowl with a fish-tailed horse flanked by figures of Eros.

And the manufacturing stamps were cool—

Ellen's voice, right behind me, startled me so that I nearly tipped over my coffee mug.

"Lisa, I really need to talk to you."

"Sure, hang on a minute. Hey, Ellen, do you remember the potsherds I told you about that show changes of ownership in Arretine factories? I want to add those to the exhibit in the section on industrial trade."

"You mean the ones with double names inscribed on them?"

"Right. The factory owner—someone like Perennius—was listed first, and his chief assistant, a slave, was listed second. When the slave became a freedman, the names were reversed. Those sherds would be perfect for the last case..."

Then I noticed Ellen's white face. "What's wrong?"

"That bitch. That hopeless bitch. I don't know what I'm going to do!" Ellen sat down with a thump on the corner of my crowded desk.

I pushed control-save on my keyboard. "Val strikes again? Of course. I'm in the same boat. That bitch, as you so rightly call her, has royally screwed up my labels. I don't know how I'm going to decipher her handwriting and finish corrections in time for new labels to be printed and dry-mounted. So, what's she done to you?"

"She took away my Getty Foundation grant! It's due tomorrow, and I just know she's going to piss all over it and demand changes so I can't possibly finish in time to make the deadline!" Ellen's blond hair stood up all over her head as if she had raked it with a garden tool. She clutched the fabric of her black pants with claw-like fingers.

"Sounds just her style. Wait, I have an idea." I leaned back in my chair, considering. "Your grant application's all online, right?"

"Yeah. What are you getting at?"

"And she took away only your printed rough draft, right?"

"Yup."

"Well, you have an option I don't with my hard-copy labels. Finish the grant your way, online, and send it in electronically. Then make the corrections on the printed copy you give Val—after the deadline. She'll never know the two copies are different because she won't see the electronic form of the grant again. It'll have disappeared into cyberspace, out of her reach."

Ellen's grin transformed her face. "You're brilliant! And a lifesaver. It's a good thing, because I was about to pick out my statue for smashing Val's smirking face. If ever someone deserved to be crushed..."

"Psychologically as well as physically. Do you suppose she ever feels remorse? Or has second thoughts of any kind?"

"No, of course not. That kind of monstrous ego never does. She probably lies awake at night planning how to make her staff members tear their hair out."

"That's a lovely image. Why don't we make a huge pile of hair..." I began.

"...and mail it to her Special Delivery." Ellen grinned triumphantly.

"Just like my favorite children's book!" I said. " 'Supposing I collected old hair from the barber and mailed it to people I didn't like.' I'm probably not quoting it right."

Ellen exploded with laughter. "No! There really is a book like that?"

"Yes. It's called *Supposing*. I'm sure it's out of print, but you can probably get it on Amazon or Alibris."

The interlude had refreshed me. "Now, scat, Ellen. I've got to finish this, and I don't have any way to fool Val with duplicate labels."

"I owe you one, Lisa. See you." Ellen's normal bounce was restored.

I groaned and returned to the tyranny of my computer. I read Val's next correction: "replace 'the red ground was the result of a three-stage firing process, oxidation-reduction-oxidation...' with 'the vase was red because it received extra air.'"

That was a ridiculous over-simplification. I would do it my way.

Sixteen

Tuesday, February 18

    The next morning, having safely dispatched her grant as an email attachment and carefully neglecting to send a copy to Val, Ellen came in early to catch up on paperwork. She crossed the "lab," an old classroom euphemistically labeled by its current function, and dumped her carryall and purse next to her antique desk, a gun-metal gray number that was a reject from some filthy rich science department on the other side of campus. On a nearby hook, Ellen hung her scruffy ankle-length down coat, the one that made her look like a duck with ruffled feathers—Lisa had nicknamed the coat the "Blue Meanie" despite the fact that she coveted it. Goose down was essential when it got this cold; Ellen didn't have the cold tolerance to wear the light jackets and flip-flops the students wore in all weather. Still wearing her boots, she stomped over to the coffee pot.

    As she filled the percolator with fresh water and turned the knob to "strong," Ellen thought about the recent interaction with Valerie. Could she have handled it differently? Stuck up for herself more effectively and refused to release the grant? Hardly, if she wanted to keep her job. She and Lisa were in the same boat; now that Dean Saltonstall had given Val his blessing and demoted Lisa, neither of them had any clout. Val now had the ability to fire either of them at whim, so they had to leap to the swing of Val's jump rope ("Hot Peppers! Faster! Faster!").

But Valerie Albrecht can't last, Ellen kept telling herself. She's bad news all around. Dean Saltonstall will certainly take notice if all the museum staff people vanish and there's no one left to complete the move to the new building. Let alone run the current museum. But who would dare tell the Dean what was really going on? Ellen had no "in" with the administration, not the way Lisa did, with her university teaching experience and her Ph.D. And everything Val had done—so far—was within her rights as the New Broom.

Ellen filled her mug with extra-strong coffee and added three teaspoons of sugar. She used Equal at home in a vain effort to curb her tendency towards plumpness, but at work she craved honest-to-god, real sugar for the energy and pseudo-sweetness of manner it produced in her.

Today she had planned to compare the registration records with Dylan's packing lists and make sure there were no gaps in their agreed-upon sequence. The remainder of the European collection was being moved this week and that included some prize acquisitions of altarpieces that Victor had arranged before his death. Wrapping her cold hands around the warm mug, she sat down in front of her monitor and typed in her password.

"Hellohellohello..." said the screen. Then it changed to "Hahahaha..."

Ellen put her mug down hastily and tapped some other commands. Nothing happened. She picked up the phone and called Dylan.

"Dylan? Have you checked your computer this morning?"

"No, I had to stop at the dry cleaner's so I just got here. What's wrong?"

"Something's taken over the whole system. Looks to me like a really nasty virus."

She listened while Dylan tapped on his keyboard.

"Sheeeit." Dylan let out a long hiss of dismay. "You're right, El. It's cooked—and we're screwed. Damn, the timing of this couldn't be worse! I'll start calling around—see if I can get someone at the Computer Clinic to help us." He hung up.

Ellen heard shuffling and turned around as Lisa entered her office. She noticed the dark circles under her friend's eyes with alarm.

"Lisa... you look like Val-the-Mack-Truck ran over you."

Lisa's lips crumpled. "You can say that again." She leaned on the edge of Ellen's desk.

Maybe a new disaster would serve as a distraction. "Hey, Lisa, look at this." Ellen slid her chair backwards so Lisa could peer at the screen.

"Uh-oh! That looks bad!"

"Did you see anything like this before you left yesterday?" Ellen asked.

Lisa frowned. "I was in no shape to notice anything when I left yesterday. I didn't even check my email on the way out. Oh, wait—did you know Georgie got fired yesterday?"

"Yes, I saw it happen."

"You did! Tell me every single gory detail."

Ellen complied. "...so he dropped a vase, and Val caught him. She threw him out so fast that he didn't even clean up his mess."

They looked at each other.

Ellen said, "It happened right at the end of the day..."

"And Val didn't tell Dylan, who is the only person now who knows how to reset the security password."

"So Georgie-Porgie got into the network and crashed it. That is, if he has enough computer savvy to do it."

"We don't know it was George, but it could have been. Dylan told me he's a whiz on the computer. If it was George, you'd better hope crashing the network temporarily was all he did. What if he corrupted the database as well?"

Ellen sagged in her seat, thinking of all those months of work.

The phone rang. Ellen picked it up.

"Someone loaded a version of the Blaster worm," Dylan told her. "And it's not just our internal network. The hacker got into our database, too. We have to go back to the last back-up disk—I think that was a week ago."

Ellen hung up and filled Lisa in. They agreed that it could have been much, much worse if they hadn't had a file back-up system in place. A week's worth of data would be a nuisance to recover, but not an impossible task.

Suddenly Ellen wondered if the cyber attack was really connected with George's dismissal.

What if it had something to do with Victor's murder, instead?

Seventeen

Wednesday, February 19

It was morning. Or was it?

I was so exhausted that I could feel my bones quivering inside their sheaths of muscle and skin. Even my clothes felt loose, as if I'd lost weight overnight. Perfectly plausible, since I couldn't remember the last time I'd had a sit-down meal. During the final race to beat the visitors to the vase exhibit opening, I had inhaled several doughnuts and a pizza or two, but nothing hot or nutritious. My abused, caffeine-addled stomach growled as I surveyed the almost finished gallery.

It was Wednesday, two days before the opening of the exhibit. The walls were tacky with fresh paint, and an army of students had just finished placing the major cases. My wall panels, fresh from the printer, awaited mounting and the object labels were mostly in place.

A sixth-grade class moved through the adjacent gallery, accompanied by several parent-chaperones who peered curiously at the roped-off area that marked the boundaries of the ceramic exhibit. I sighed, relieved that it was almost over—Friday night was almost upon us.

Just then I heard Val's high heels click-clacking down the hall. I tensed, wondering if I'd compromised a bit too much on the labels.

The heels stopped near my right foot.

"Well, it looks nice, Lisa. I see you've got the new labels done on time."

No thanks to you, bitch.

Val peered into a case illustrating Greek firing technologies. "Now wait a minute." She'd zeroed in on the red-figured amphora depicting a potter's workshop. "I distinctly remember telling you to revise that label." Val's lips thinned into a bloodless squiggle as she radiated outrage.

"I did modify it, Val, but I also shortened it. As curator for the show, I thought that—"

"Curator?" Valerie said in a biting voice so loud that every student and chaperone in the armor display turned our way. "Everything we do in the museum is a team effort, you know that. And everything written by *any* of the staff gets edited by me!"

I could feel the heat rise up my chest and neck. "When Victor assigned me this show..."

"Victor, Victor!" shrieked Valerie, stomping her expensive Italian heel on the floor. "Your former boss is dead, dear, and I'm in charge of this show, this museum! And your position here is *temporary*." She shoved her pointy nose almost into mine.

Out of the corner of my eye, I could see Susie, Dylan, and Sara at the far end of the gallery. Their motionless stances indicated that they were listening avidly.

"Valerie, this is hardly the ideal place—couldn't we move to your office if you want to discuss this?" I hated the fact that my voice sounded pleading and childish.

"We'll discuss it right here, Lisa, while I review your work." Valerie strutted over to the next case. "Pull out your notebook. You're going to fix every label if you know what's good for you. And look, here's a typo, we can't have that!"

Val's penetrating voice pounded away as I stood rooted to the dusty floor. This couldn't be happening. Being screamed at by a psycho boss in front of my peers and the general public? Hot tears rose behind my eyelids as I struggled for control.

I will not cry. I will not cry.

"Lisa," Val continued in that fruity, condescending voice I despised, "You can't have the focal point of your exhibit be a kiln model. We need a major artifact under this spotlight, here, to draw people in to the exhibit."

"But this is what we agreed upon, and the exhibit opening is in barely forty-eight hours!"

Valerie's hazel eyes turned into laser beams. "You're not listening, Lisa. You need to move that large *krater* over here, and shift the kiln set-up into that corner." She waved her hand casually, having no idea how long it had taken us to arrange the current display.

I said, "If we change the exhibit layout now, the sequence of labels will be messed up! There isn't time..."

"Lisa, I remember telling you I might make changes at any time. Give me the layout diagram."

I handed it over with great reluctance. Val had had many opportunities to change the layout before now. But planning ahead wasn't how she operated. Now that Val was the boss, she exulted in changing things at the worst possible time and making the staff scramble to accommodate her whims.

Val progressed around the gallery, drawing X's and arrows with her big, red marker all over my carefully drawn plans.

My stomach did dips and dives every time Valerie made a change, and I could feel my blood beginning to curdle as rage built up inside me. I'd give anything to throw a bucket of water over Val, the Wicked Witch of the West, and have her disappear into nothingness: *"I'm melting, I'm melting! Who would have thought a little girl like you could destroy my beautiful wickedness?"* Water vapor would rise from Val's black robes, until all that was left was the pointed hat. Goodbye, Wicked Witch, good riddance. Or maybe I could just drop a house on her, like Dorothy... then I could report to an admiring Wizard of Oz (Dean Saltonstall): "I liquidated her." And he would reply, just like Oz, "How resourceful of you."

My lovely fantasy ended abruptly as Valerie handed me the mangled exhibit plans, saying, "Fix it, Lisa. You haven't got much time. And by the way, I won't be in tomorrow. I'll take another look at the exhibit on Friday morning." Val swept out of the gallery like royalty, leaving me stranded like a girl at a bus stop right after the last school bus has pulled away.

She can't do this to me! Miserable, heartless bitch!

As I crept back to my office, my brain began a frantic reassessment. I'd have to find some way to compromise between the original layout and what Val wanted. Could I move a couple of cases and rearrange the wall panels so the sequence of information still made sense? Val had kept no copy of her revisions—with luck, she wouldn't remember all the details of what she had ordered me to do.

Dream on, sweetheart.

That didn't change the fact that I was in for a very long night. James would be pissed—the fourth late night in the past ten days. But with his crazy schedule, he ought to understand.

I trudged past the gift shop, wishing that for once I had noisy, clacking shoes to express my frustration. My soft-soled Hush Puppies made only dull thuds—totally unsatisfactory.

Viciously, I pushed over a chair as I passed the deserted front desk, reveling in the crash it made.

Maybe a good witch would furnish me with ruby slippers, and James and I could get out of Oz.

Eighteen

Same day, afternoon

"You mean she trashed your whole exhibit plan *two days before the Opening?*" Ellen asked, leaning back against the ancient green couch. "I don't believe it!" She and I were alone in the cluttered attic room we called our staff lounge.

"And how. I'll have to get help tonight to rearrange everything. Can you stay late?" I filled my coffee mug and sank into a nearby armchair, the one with a large tear in the seat cover.

"I guess so. What a pain, though. I think we should rename Val 'Livia.'"

"Livia as in *'I Claudius'*? I was thinking of her as the Wicked Witch of the West, but Livia is even better." The wife of the Roman emperor Augustus as portrayed in the PBS special was a manipulative, scheming tyrant. Livia made her relatives dance like puppets on their strings, doing her will without being aware that she controlled their movements. Very much like Val. The difference here was that at least two of Val's puppets knew we were having our strings tangled up. And our psyches dangled, dropped, and trampled upon.

Ellen slumped lower into the couch, trying to merge into a cushion.

I changed the subject—I'd be there all night, I could afford to spend ten minutes chatting with my best friend. "Things going okay with Dylan?"

"Yeah. Well, most of the time. He's so preoccupied these days—he's not even interested in trying out new recipes. Last night I made a really boring macaroni and cheese casserole."

I smiled. Mac and cheese—with leftover veggies—was a regular dinner option at our house. "Well, we have this new deadline on the packing and moving, and an ongoing murder investigation doesn't help." I noticed that the tiny lines around Ellen's lips were deeper than usual and that under her eyes were gray shadows that owed nothing to make-up. "There's something else, isn't there?"

Ellen looked up, and I was startled to see tears gathering in Ellen's bright blue eyes. "I overheard Valerie coming on to Dylan. And he seemed pretty responsive."

"Oh, no! What did you hear, exactly?"

"It was a couple of days ago, in her office. Val was admiring Dylan's arm muscles—he works out, you know, at that new twenty-four hour gym on Boylston—and he was lapping it up. Boasting about which exercises worked best and so on. I peeked in the door, and she had sidled up close and was feeling his biceps."

"Why didn't you just barge in and disrupt their little party?" I leaned forward.

"I wanted to see what he'd do next," Ellen said bitterly. "He just stood there, and then I heard her invite him out for a drink after work."

"And?"

"He murmured some sort of protest, but then she said something that made him pull back and say, 'the hell you would!'"

I frowned. "Sounds like a little pressure from the lady."

"Lady!" sneered Ellen. "That bitch is no lady!"

"We all know that. So did he go out with her?"

Ellen started crying in earnest. "I don't know! I had to work late, and I haven't gotten up the nerve to ask him!" She punched the pillow next to her.

I crossed to the couch and put an arm around my weeping friend. I thought fondly of strangling Val, thus solving Ellen's problems as well as my own. But strangling was too good for someone who deliberately caused as much harm as possible. Boiling in oil—that would be better. Or maybe a slow death by poison, the sort that made you writhe and froth at the mouth?

I remembered another young man at my first museum in Philadelphia. Brad something. An anthropology student with a roving eye and a sleek, compact physique—just Val's type. Brad had been promoted rather quickly over staff members who had M.A.s and PhDs because he had buttered up Val, joking and flirting with her at every opportunity.

"Ellen," I began, trying to think how best to say the unpleasant truths that Ellen didn't want to hear. "Maybe this is a blessing in disguise. If Dylan is messing around with your boss, right under your nose, then he's not worth the jeans he's wearing. You should dump him and get on with your life."

"But I really like him!" Ellen sobbed, curling up into a tight little ball on the worn green couch that had witnessed so many staff meltdowns. "And besides, he's fantastic in bed!"

I grimaced. I really didn't want to hear any sordid details about Dylan's sexual prowess. A man who prided himself on his skill in bed—one who cut a notch on a metaphorical stick for each conquest—was about as appealing as a cockroach.

I rubbed Ellen's shoulders until her tears slowed to a trickle. "You need to confront him. Find out what's really going on. And then, if he really is cheating on you, get the hell out. For your own mental health." And physical health, I added silently. I suspected that Dylan was promiscuous or even bisexual; he was probably a good candidate for getting AIDS.

Ellen dragged herself to a sitting position and groped in her pocket for a clean tissue. She mopped her eyes and took a deep breath. "You're right, of course. But thinking about breaking up with him and actually going through with it are two different things."

"Just concentrate on what it will be like to go on ski weekends in Vermont again. Dylan hates skiing—you told me that—and you adore it. Remember the fondue place at Stowe? You can treat yourself to all three kinds of fondue: meat, cheese, and chocolate. How's that for motivation?"

Ellen grinned, her natural balance restored. "Chocolate is better than sex anyhow." She hugged me. "Thanks, Lise. You've proved you're worth your weight in..."

"Gold. Yes, I know."

"I was going to say, 'lead.'"

"Jeez! Just because I've gained a couple of pounds this winter, there's no reason to..."

"I'm kidding!" Ellen laughed at me.

"Oh, right. I'll get you for that," I said.

I hugged Ellen and headed back to the exhibit gallery.

Nineteen

Friday, February 21

Somehow it all came together, as it always did.

Everyone helped. Nancy showed an unexpected talent for trouble-shooting on the computer and Ellen rearranged cases with artistic flair. Even Dylan showed up and cheerfully moved ladders and mounted wall panels at my request. No one went home until after two am on the day of the Opening.

Luckily for me, Val had never bothered to check on the exhibit one last time as she'd threatened. Now it was Friday evening; our hard work was over and our guests were arriving. The paint gleamed under the track lighting, and the buffet tables—sawhorses and board tables swiped from Registration and disguised by slightly yellowed white tablecloths—looked sumptuous.

I planned to drown my bone-deep fatigue in champagne and yummy goodies from University Catering: meatballs, eggplant dip with Italian bread, cute little ham sandwiches, goat cheese toasts... As I sipped my second glass of fizz, I looked at a freshly redone label and gasped as I noticed a typo—hardly a surprise, with all the last minute changes.

Susie, who looked as if she'd been poured into her gold brocade gown and matching shoes, glided up to me. "Congratulations, Lisa. I bet you sleep well tonight!"

"I wish I could be sure of that. But I keep noticing things we missed in the mad rush. Val will take it out on me when she finds out it's not perfect."

Susie's brown eyebrows lowered. "That woman is heading for an accident—a permanent one."

I smiled. "You've already picked out a statue for her, haven't you?" Then, as Susie gave me a strange look, I realized that my remark was an exceedingly tactless reminder of how Victor had died.

Hastily, I changed the subject. "Who's the new guy?"

"I don't know who you mean."

"The skinny guy popping champagne corks."

Susie turned away. "Probably some grad student friend of Dylan's helping out. Hey, have you tried the steamed salmon with dill sauce, sour cream, and capers yet? It's divine."

As I watched her mincing down the gallery in her high heels, I saw Val schmoozing with a wealthy donor, a Mr. Whitehill. Val was gesticulating in graceful swoops with one hand, and the guy was clearly fascinated. They drew another well-nourished, tuxedoed man into their orbit and Val continued to dominate the conversation. I had to admit she was awfully good at getting donors committed to the museum.

Then Val paused, her attention caught by something in the exhibit case closest to her.

Uh oh. She's noticed something wrong.

Well. After the last public dressing-down, I'd vowed that the next time Val pulled a stunt like that, I would leave the room. Or do something drastic, like scream or stick my finger down my throat and vomit. Preferably all over Val's Italian shoes.

Or I could resign—but that would give Val a major victory. Besides, my gut said, "don't give up, it's too soon." I had far too much invested in this job.

Could Valerie Albrecht really last more than six months as Director? I'd heard rumors among my faculty friends that Val was making enemies left, right, and center. And our museum wasn't a private institution—it was a university unit, subject to faculty review. The faculty would be very hard on a museum director who wasn't serving their interests. So, as several of us had agreed, all we had to do was tough it out.

Ellen, looking delicious in a dark blue silk skirt with a white lace top, distracted me by appearing at my elbow.

"Hey, Lisa! We survived, right?"

"Yeah. Only now I'm worried because I saw Val reacting like a hunting dog to something in the kiln display. I bet she's found an error."

"Well, whatever it is, I'm sure the boom won't lower until Monday, so you can enjoy your champagne." She craned her neck to see where Valerie was. "Oh, no."

The crowd parted to reveal Val, complete with donor entourage, advancing purposefully toward me.

"Lisa! I just noticed you changed the fonts on the labels. In fact, it looks like you ignored all my instructions!" Val's voice rose. "I demand to know what happened, right now!"

I willed my heart rate to slow down. "Val, we can't discuss this here." Dimly, I noticed a small crowd gathering nearby. "I'd be happy to explain everything on Monday—"

"You'll explain here and now!"

A man in a dark suit and cropped white hair standing behind Val turned towards us. Dean Saltonstall.

Adrenaline and champagne made me reckless. I raised my voice slightly so everyone in the vicinity could hear. "As I was saying, Val, this is hardly the time or place to discuss label corrections. I was planning to tell you exactly what happened at nine am on Monday, in your office. But since you've insisted on an explanation now—with all these kind folks listening in, here it is—the reason why the labels look different is because you made all those changes less than forty-eight hours before the exhibit. Then you went home, leaving me in charge. Naturally, Printing Services was unable to accommodate us, so we created the labels in house, on our own state-of-the-art printer. Just the way we planned to when I was Interim Director. Now, if you'll excuse me, I see some Friends of the Museum who need to be welcomed."

I locked gazes briefly with the Dean, who stiffened. I spun around to face the newcomers standing next to the mound of salmon on the refreshments table.

As I walked away, praying I wouldn't trip and fall on my posterior, an ominous murmur rose behind me.

Good job, Lisa, Now you've really done it.

~ * ~

I took a taxi home.

In my current shattered state of mind, I couldn't bear to take the subway. Besides, my feet in my slick new shoes were killing me. What had possessed me to think that two-inch heels would suit me when they never had before? And in February! From behind, I probably looked like an inebriated stork.

I paid off the taxi driver and teetered up the brick steps to our front door. Only Oreo was at home to greet me; James had taken Sam and Emma to the latest Tolkien movie. By now, they should be up to their ears in Orc blood and the long march of Frodo and Sam to Mt. Doom. Bully for them.

Mt. Doom—now that was an image. A spitting volcano was not a bad analogy for Val, now that she'd been humiliated in public. A small, mean part of me was glad I'd done it, but the rest of me acknowledged the very hollow feeling such a "triumph" produced in the pit of my stomach. What good did it do to win one round with Val when the consequences would surely be either the loss of my job or, at the very least, a much more stressful workplace?

I kicked off the offending shoes, reflecting that the heels would make a dandy weapon for smashing up someone's face, and poured a glass of Chardonnay. As soon as I slid into a kitchen chair, Oreo jumped up and kneaded himself a nest in my lap, purring like a lawnmower. One of his claws caught in the silk fabric of my little black dress, distracting me from my gloomy thoughts until I untangled his paw and we both settled down.

Patting the cat, who responded with enthusiastic rumbles and rolling over to display his black and white tummy, calmed me enough for my brain to function again. James would probably be relieved if I lost my job; then I could spend more time with Sam and Emma—and maybe the refrigerator would be stocked more often. To James' credit, he'd try to hide his relief and be very sympathetic about the derailment of my career.

On the other hand—there was always another point of view. My father, an ex-lawyer, had taught me that when he helped me with my math homework. Instead of showing me one easy way to do it, he'd suggest three different solutions. Maybe that was why I had so much trouble with moral dilemmas—I always saw multiple shades of gray instead of just black and white.

I'd invested so much in my identity as a museum professional. I loved museum work. Everything about it excited me, especially the transforming of esoteric research into accessible wall texts, artifact labels, and catalogues that the museum-going public could understand and enjoy. For the first time in ages, I admitted to myself how much ambition I still had. I really wanted to push myself to be the best curator I could be. And I felt regret that I hadn't been allowed to really test myself in the Director's position. I knew this was a job I could do well, given time.

A key turned in the lock.

"Mommy! You're home early!" cried Emma as she bounced into the living room.

"You missed an awesome battle! You should have seen the elephants and the war machines and the Orcs..." Sam was ecstatic.

I smiled weakly and dumped the cat on the floor so I could hug them both.

James regarded me thoughtfully. "You don't seem to have your normal post-Opening euphoria. What happened?"

I sighed. "Val bawled me out in public—in front of several major donors and the Dean—for changing the label printing style."

His bushy eyebrows shot up. "I bet that went over well! What did you do?"

"I told the truth—that she'd made a gazillion changes at the very last minute, ruling out using the Campus Printing Services so that we had to produce the labels in-house using our own computers and printers. I also said it was inappropriate to have that sort of discussion between staff members at a museum social function."

"Whew! And David Saltonstall was right there?" James popped the top off a bottle of Sam Adams beer and took a healthy swig.

"Yeah. He looked kinda stunned—I've no idea what he thought. "Or what he's going to do, I added silently.

Emma butted up against me for another hug and then ran to the refrigerator to forage for a snack. James handed her two granola bars. "Give one to Sam. I'll pour you guys some milk in a minute. Why don't you go upstairs and let me talk to Mom?"

The kids vanished, and soon thumping noises indicated they were above us.

"You're worried about your job, aren't you?" James said.

We talked it over, and I aired all my fears. James certainly had issues with me getting involved in amateur sleuthing, but he'd always been supportive about my career. I knew—and was often reminded—that I was extraordinarily lucky to have such a husband.

"James. If I do lose the job, how would you feel if I applied for teaching jobs?"

"Think you could get one in the Boston area?"

I crossed to the sink and poured myself some water to chase the wine. "Yes—as long as I included community colleges in the search. It couldn't pay any worse than a museum job—might even pay better."

James nodded. "Then how can you lose? It might be a good change for you—being your own boss most of the time instead of answering to the likes of Valerie." He smiled ruefully. "It's rather like my fantasy of taking an academic job for a while—getting out of the hospital environment."

Not really listening to him, I said, "There's only one problem."

"What's that?"

"I really love the museum work."

James pulled me down into the chair next to him and enfolded me in a bear hug. He rested his bearded chin on the top of my head. I let out a long sigh.

We rested together in the crowded little kitchen, leaning together like books on a shelf.

~ * ~

Ellen called Sunday night while I was emptying the dishwasher.

"Lisa? Sorry I didn't call sooner. I went up to my parents' cottage in Portland. So, what kind of weekend did you have after telling Val off?"

"Okay, I guess," I said. "But I'm afraid I'm going to get fired."

"I very much doubt that. Don't you want to hear what happened after you left the Opening?"

"You're going to tell me whether I like it or not."

Ellen laughed. "Wow, that was some scene! I thought the Dean was going to explode!"

I continued to stack dishes on the counter with the phone wedged between my face and shoulder. "What did he do? And what did Val do?"

"He said something to Val that made her turn white. She started to sputter. Then the Dean grabbed her arm and pulled her off to one side. From what I could see, he told her off like a misbehaving child."

"She'll find some way to take that out on me—I just know it."

"Maybe," said Ellen with a lilt to her voice. "But you'll still have your job. I overheard Dean Saltonstall say, 'You can't fire her. I won't let you.'"

I stood motionless, a plastic glass in my hand. "Holy Cow!"

"'Course he didn't say she had to keep you in exactly the same position. She'll probably find some way to demote you, or otherwise make your life a hell."

"Thanks for nothing."

Ellen's voice was warm and bracing. "Whatever she does, just ride it out. You'll come out on top, because Val's bad behavior is definitely causing comments. She can't last."

An echo of what I'd thought: she can't last.

And then little cold fingers brushed my spine.

Twenty

Friday, February 28

A few days later, I trudged through slush and old dog poop on the way to work. I hated February, hated my job, and most of all, I wanted my horrible boss to simply disappear.

The atmosphere at the museum since the Opening could only be described as... anticipatory. Everyone who'd witnessed Val's outrageous behavior and my spirited response was eagerly waiting for the next installment. As dirty water splattered on my lined raincoat from a passing car, I tried to cheer myself up by thinking of soap opera titles: "Happy Days in A Derelict Museum," "Days of Our Lives—In Hell," or "Lost in the Secret Attic." No, that last one sounded too much like the Nancy Drew mystery.

I unlocked the back door to the museum and started up the back stairs. Instantly, I had a flashback to the last time I'd had to close the museum after dark. Our crowded attic galleries were a challenge to navigate in full daylight. At night, odd noises emerged from the ancient heating system, and pigeons cooed in the eaves or flew in and out of the broken windows. With the lights off, the museum was positively spooky.

It didn't help my mood that McEwan wasn't talking to me. As I'd expected, he'd been very interested in the attack on the museum's computer system. But all my recent information was secondhand. According to Ellen, who'd overhead as McEwan reported to Val, he was not at all sure it was just a revenge stunt by George Skirvin; if Victor's murderer had done it, he argued, then there must be something on the museum's computers that was incriminating to him or her. McEwan's team was spending hours with Dylan and Ellen, delving into all their computer security procedures. So far, they'd found exactly nothing.

Nor was my humble home a refuge because Sam had gotten worse. This week, even the mention of school made his little face grow pale with apprehension. I'd tried coaxing the real reason Sam hated school out of him—I was sure there was one—but Sam had stubbornly refused to say anything.

I'd met with the teacher, Miss Edwards, thinking perhaps Sam was afraid of her. Picturing a middle-aged ogre who believed in military discipline, I was surprised to encounter a fresh-faced kid with curly dark hair and a riveting smile. She looked, and probably was, about twenty-two.

"Sam's last report card was okay. Is he having problems paying attention in class?" I asked.

"No, that's not it," Miss Edwards replied. "He listens, does his assignments, but his heart's not in it. Last semester, he was my most engaged student—always raising his hand and asking questions."

I cast around for another explanation. "What about his friends? Everything okay there?"

The teacher grinned. "I have a pack of boys who run around together during recess. As far as I can tell, Sam is always in the thick of things."

"Well, something's bothering him. Any ideas?"

Miss Edwards brushed her curls back self-consciously. "Maybe he still misses his dead mother. Perhaps he hasn't adjusted to the idea of a stepmother?"

I'd gritted my teeth and said, no, the relationship between Sam and his stepmother was fine, thank you *very* much.

And then I wondered. Was Sam secretly comparing me to his dead mother, Carol Barber? Did I fail to measure up in the mothering department, in how I nuked cheese-filled tortillas, or told nighttime stories? James was no help—he thought everything was hunky-dory, at least when he had time to think about anything except the relentless demands of his new job as department head.

I'd arrived at the rear entrance of the museum, the gloomy anteroom that used to be our European gallery. I flicked on the lights and made tracks for the alarm switchboard. After flicking a series of old-fashioned switches from "on" to "off," I called Campus Security and gave my password, which was "Athena." That's right, I was the Greek goddess of wisdom, who'd sprung fully armed from the head of Zeus. This phone call prompted the usual response, "Right, Miz Donahue," and a deep chuckle from the cop on duty. I shed my boots on the mat so I could carry them into my office without making unsightly puddles on the gallery floors.

I'd barely unbuttoned my L.L. Bean fleece jacket when Dylan arrived.

"Guess what?"

"Oh, hell. Another floor crack?"

"Yup. A huge one this time. Sounded like a minor earthquake."

I put my jacket back on. "I guess you'd better show me."

Dylan and I walked briskly across campus to the new building. Dylan's hair was sleeked back from his shapely head, and his bicep muscles bulged even under the light windbreaker he was wearing. Eyeing his trim physique and tight butt, I could see why Ellen found him attractive.

Too bad his personality didn't match the nice bod. Or maybe it was just bad chemistry—nothing about Dylan sparked my interest on a visceral level. But he could be a charming conversationalist.

Now he was talking about food, which he adored both as a chef and as an enthusiastic consumer.

"It had eggplant with roasted garlic and red peppers, and I added herbed goat cheese when I served it. Ellen and I having been eating more vegetarian lately," Dylan said.

Hmm. Dylan and Ellen were still cooking together, whatever was going on between Dylan and Val. And Dylan certainly preferred to talk about cooking rather than the online museum studies course he was taking. Was he doing any of the reading?

I pretended enthusiasm to keep the conversation going. "Have you tried any more pasta dishes lately?"

"Oh, sure! I invented one with porcini mushrooms and Asiago cheese."

I remembered the pasta dish with the Mediterranean sauce James and I had eaten at Dylan and Ellen's apartment on Valentine's Day. I had to admit Dylan was a good cook—if only he didn't sound so puffed up about it. And his kitchen! Dylan insisted on organizing it the way most men arranged their shops—all his favorite tools in handy places. And they were the very latest in kitchen gadgets. I suspected that Ellen—a mean chef in her own right when she had the time—had been demoted to dishwashing since she started dating Dylan. And naturally she had moved in with him, rather than the other way around. Dylan couldn't leave his kitchen.

"Dylan, how's the museum studies course going?"

"Oh, fine. They send me a packet of readings every two weeks. It's a little hard to keep up and work full-time," he said airily.

Uh-huh. At least he was trying. "Which university is it?"

"Leicester, in England. I'm supposed to finish in another semester."

We arrived at the new Edward G. Taylor museum building before Dylan had finished describing his wine selections for both the pasta and the eggplant dishes. He led the way to the new Ancient Mediterranean gallery and took a dramatic stance with his right hand pointed at the floor.

I stood in appalled silence. The new crack zigzagged across the middle of the "holding room," the space we'd designated for school groups to gather and hear the tourguide's introduction to the gallery. In this case, it was also the space where we wanted guests to circulate during the Grand Opening of the new museum.

"Did the contractor give you any explanation?" Frantically, I wondered how I'd explain this latest delay to Val without getting my head snapped off. I'd been pleased that Val allowed me to continue as the museum's liaison with the architect; normally that was a job the new Director would have assumed. But I was uncomfortably aware of Val's strategy. If anything went wrong, she'd make sure the Dean knew, and he'd take me apart. Or, on second thought, maybe not—he might blast Val for delegating the wrong duties.

"Gene said something about the material of the faux-sandstone coating not bonding properly to the substrate cement—whatever that means."

I said, "You'd think a campus with a world-class engineering program could manage floor construction, wouldn't you?"

Dylan laughed. "One hand doesn't know what the other is doing—you know that. Besides, didn't the University hire outside contractors for the flooring?"

"Yeah, you're right." Another fire to put out, and I was so far behind on my teaching preparations. Why had I agreed to teach a course next semester, anyway? I must be masochistic, overloading myself like this.

Dylan eyed the crack again. "You know," he said thoughtfully, "it doesn't matter if they can't fix it in time for the Grand Opening. If we placed the buffet tables diagonally and placed some potted plants strategically at each end, no one would even notice it."

I gazed at him in genuine admiration. They'd have to be fake potted plants because we couldn't introduce molds and insects into the new museum if we wanted to meet national accreditation standards, but it would work. "Dylan, that's brilliant! Now I know what to tell Val."

Dylan patted my shoulder and smiled.

Smarmy, smug bastard, I thought. But smart—very smart.

~ * ~

After lunch, I was updating my "to do" list on my computer when I heard light footsteps. I glanced up from my keyboard and saw Sara Browning standing hesitantly in the doorway of my office. I motioned to the only chair that didn't have piles of paper on it, and returned to my computer and hit "save." When I turned around the second time, I found Sara perched on the edge of the chair, chewing the ends of her long, brown hair.

Sara blushed and whipped the hair out of her mouth.

Huh. Sara had better quit that habit or she'd end up with a hairball in her stomach, like a cat. James had told me a story—a true one—about a young teenager who'd had an operation after cannibalizing her own braids. The surgeon had found both hair and the fabric scrunchy used to fasten it inside the girl's stomach.

I smiled and leaned back in my chair, hoping to relax her. "What's up?"

"Well, I—I'm not sure. Something odd happened, and I thought I should tell someone..." Sara's lustrous Bambi-like eyes, enhanced with just the right amount of dark brown mascara, opened wider.

Another shy person who might flee at the first hint of a loud voice, I thought, waiting.

"You know how Dylan is in charge of the packing for the move?" Sara blushed as she spoke Dylan's name.

I nodded. Poor Sara. She didn't stand a chance with Dylan while both Ellen and Val were in the picture.

"Well, I went down to the loading area on the first floor to give him a new list of artifacts for the next truckload, and he wasn't there. There was a guy in an Operations and Maintenance uniform moving one of our loaded carts into the freight elevator. A tall, thinnish guy, someone I've never seen before. I asked him who he was, and he said Steve Something, just helping Dylan out with the move."

"That's odd."

And it made me uneasy. Was it the same guy I'd seen at the Greek vase exhibit opening? We were still in the middle of moving some forty-five thousand artifacts to the new building. When Victor was still alive, we'd agreed not to accept help from anyone outside our department. The fewer people who knew how valuable some of the artifacts were, the better. Had Dylan been hiring people without going through me or the Dean?

My pulse quickened. What if this new guy was absconding with Celtic artifacts? If he was, he must be working with someone on the staff who knew the collections. If Dylan had hired him, then Dylan was the most likely suspect for Chief Thief. Or maybe it was Tim Marsden, who'd completed a great deal of research on the European and Celtic materials as part of his thesis preparation.

Sara interrupted my train of thought. "The new guy was kind of surly. Like he didn't want to answer my questions. And I thought about the Bryn Mawr Torque disappearing and thought I should tell someone."

"You did the right thing, Sara. I'll look into it. And I've got to spend more time in the basement; I've never visited some of those storerooms. Aren't there tunnels between buildings, too? I don't even know exactly what we have down there."

I was exaggerating. Of course I knew roughly what was down there—it was part of my job as a curator. Our museum had never had enough storage space—that's why we were moving to a new building with state-of-the-art moveable storage shelves and fancy new drawers of multiple sizes. In the meantime, we had some older collections that were part of the old catalogue—the kind done on yellowed index cards, in pen and pencil back in the 1930s—in basement storerooms. After the major move, probably well into the next semester, these older collections would be moved into the new storage facilities and all the data would be entered into our spiffy new computer database.

The basement of Wigglesworth Hall was a labyrinth, with storerooms belonging to us and to at least two other departments such as Sociology and Anthropology. The other rooms were utility closets and caches of equipment for Operations and Maintenance. Did anyone on our staff have a floor plan? I didn't think so.

"Dylan has the keys," said Sara. "I know where he keeps them."

Well, well. Was Sara hinting that Dylan didn't always carry his keys on his belt and that Sara thought we could borrow them without asking him?

"Do you know your way around down there?" I asked.

Sara nodded. "Not the storerooms, but a couple of the tunnels. Last semester, my boyfriend Brian showed me how to get from Fremont Hall to the main kitchen. The main tunnel is how they transport food from dorm to dorm. He said you can go almost anywhere on campus without going outside."

"Must be handy during the winter." I remembered my own undergraduate days on another campus, where we'd used the food tunnels to sneak back to the women's dorm after the midnight curfew. The same tunnels had suddenly become less attractive when a serial rapist had roamed the interconnecting laundry rooms in the basement.

I checked my desk calendar. It was covered with scribbled notes in various colors, red being the most dominant. I had a meeting with Valerie in an hour, then coffee scheduled with Dennis Thompson about co-teaching our course. Aloud I said, "I wish we could go right now, but I can't. Do you have some time Monday or Tuesday?"

"Sure," said Sara. She stepped delicately, like a doe in search of tender leaves to munch on, through the forest of file boxes on my floor. I really hated to see someone with Sara's vulnerability in this environment. If Valerie didn't hunt her down and carve her up, then Dylan would.

Suddenly Sara turned around. "I forgot to tell you—Ellen wants you to stop in. She thinks there's another box of artifacts missing."

Oh, great. Another theft was just what I needed to make my day.

~ * ~

Ellen twirled the microscope knobs, her shoulders hunched with concentration. She frowned as she focused on the surface of an iron buckle from our Merovingian collection.

"Boy, that's a lot of corrosion," I said.

"You can say that again. I'm hoping we can X-ray this buckle. A team at the University of Illinois did that with one of their Merovingian pieces and found fantastic silver damascening decoration under all the crud."

"What's damascening?"

"Well the term is used in different ways, but in this case it means carving grooves in the iron substrate and laying silver wires in them."

"Sounds gorgeous. You wanted to see me?"

"Yeah. Hang on a sec. I'm just finishing this conservation report." Ellen scribbled in the notebook next to her and flipped it shut with a flourish.

"Sara said you're missing some more artifacts." My stomach sank even as I said the words out loud.

Ellen swiveled her chair around and gestured towards another chair. "Yup, it's only one, but it's a biggie. There's a box with an exquisite bronze Celtic cauldron that I tracked only last week. First, I saw the box in Registration, then I saw it on a cart ready to be moved into the basement—and then it vanished."

"You set up the system we talked about, for tracking each box?"

"That was the easy part. The tough part is so many people are involved in each stage of the move. It doesn't help that all our students are part-time, with crazy schedules that change on a weekly basis. I tried color-coding the boxes along with my own numbering system, but the other problem is that I'm just not there watching all the time. All it takes is one guy or gal moving a box from one cart to another and the whole system is screwed."

"Hmm. So, how many boxes are missing now?"

"There are four or five that didn't end up in the basement staging area the way they were supposed to."

"So someone is moving them out of the queue, either upstairs in the museum, or on the way to the basement."

"I vote for the basement," Ellen said. "Do you have any idea how many rooms with unmarked doors there are down there? I don't even know which department owns half of them, let alone who has keys. I only know the rooms we have for old collection storage."

My head began to ache. What Ellen said fit in with Sara's report. "Somehow, I need to find the time to go down there, snoop around a bit."

Ellen eyed me skeptically. "And when are you going to tell McEwan we have some more missing artifacts?"

"We don't know for certain that they're missing—they may just be mislaid."

"Oh, come on, Lisa!"

I groaned.

"You still have to tell him," Ellen said with a stern look.

My shoulders slumped. "You're right, of course. But we'll look like awful fools if we report stolen artifacts and then 'find' them again in one of our own basement storerooms! Besides, McEwan's left me out of the loop on this investigation. Somehow, I thought that no matter what Saltonstall or Valerie decided, he had a mind of his own and would do as he pleased. I'm going to snoop a little myself, and then I'll tell McEwan."

"I betcha he'll come around and include you again. And don't go snooping around alone," Ellen said. "Remember, there's still a murderer on the loose. Don't make it easy for him—or her."

"I was planning on going with Sara—turns out her boyfriend gave her a tour of the tunnels."

Ellen raised one blond eyebrow.

"Besides, if I get myself killed," I said, "it will save Valerie the bother."

"You don't really mean that, Lise," said my best friend. "And we *need* to bother Val. Remember that bumper sticker: 'Live long enough to be a burden to your children'?"

"Ha-ha."

Twenty-one

Monday, March 3

At the beginning of the following week, Ellen's prediction came true. I found a phone message asking me to meet McEwan in Eddie's Diner, across the street from the museum.

I was snowed under with work, behind on everything. But the thought of Eddie's wonderful, full-bodied Italian roast coffee and a chance to pick McEwan's brain was inducement enough to get me across the street in record time. My "to do" list—littered with last minute demands from Val—could wait.

McEwan slouched at the counter, stirring his brew. His eyebrows shot up as he saw me. "Italian roast, super strong, for the lady," he told Eddie, putting a couple of bills on the counter.

Eddie, a skinny guy in a white apron, handed me the aromatic coffee in a thick white mug. I inhaled it greedily and pinned McEwan with a look. "So, I assume the free caffeine is to soften me up so I'll give you information?

And ordering my favorite brew is payback for almost ignoring me these past few weeks?"

He choked on his coffee. "No one could ignore you, Ms. Donahue. I've been busy—and that new boss of yours told me to stay clear of you. I had no intention of obeying her, but I waited until today when she's in a long meeting to bring you up to date." The sergeant brushed back his graying hair and gave me a shrewd once over. "Seems she finds you threatening—why, I can't imagine—so I thought I'd avoid causing you additional grief if I pretended to do things her way."

Ellen would be proud of him. That's just how she and I operated to get around Val. I relaxed and carried my coffee over to an empty table. "Tell me what's new, then."

He pulled out a chair and sat down with a thump. "Okay, we still haven't solved Victor's murder. I want to reexamine all the possible suspects—staff members who had a grudge against Victor. Let's go back to Ms. Susie Blake."

"Why? Have you got something on her?"

"You could say that," smirked McEwan. He leaned forward to observe my reaction. "Victor *was* dating another woman."

"He *was*? Who?"

"Diana Huntington-Williams. The new Director of the Museum of Fine Arts. They were seen having dinner together at Café Louis on Berkeley St."

"Sure it was a date? Maybe it was just a business meeting between museum directors."

"Hmm," said McEwan, slurping his coffee. "Our witness said they seemed lovey-dovey, but that could be an exaggeration."

"Have you asked Susie about it?" I asked, thinking that Susie would go ballistic.

"Oh, yeah. She turned purple and said how dare Victor take anyone else to her favorite restaurant."

I chuckled. "That sounds like her. But Susie wouldn't kill Victor because he had a single date with another woman. She'd probably retaliate by inviting him over for a really intimate dinner." I didn't bother telling him what Susie would be wearing. I'd seen Susie's closet—it had a number of slinky outfits including a couple of classic négligées, complete with feather trim and matching mules.

"Still," began McEwan, but just then his cell phone rang. His face turned rigid as he listened. "Are you sure?"

I waited, mug suspended in midair.

McEwan flipped the cell shut and stared at his hands. Slowly he raised his chin and gazed at me. "That was the metal analysis report."

He radiated disbelief and something else—anger?

"And?"

He blew out between his teeth. "Victor Fitzgerald wasn't murdered after all. Lab says the steel cable suffered metal fatigue. Stress corrosion, they called it. It was an accident, pure and simple."

I whistled under my breath. "I thought it was the clamp, not the cable."

"Yeah, so did I. We thought someone had loosened the clamps, but the report says that instead, the cable itself had microscopic stress fractures above the clamp assembly. These accumulate in the material over time, waiting for a final stress to cause a break."

"So the weight of the statue and the seesaw motion of the platform going down the elevator were too much?"

"Looks that way."

"But wait a minute—shouldn't you be able to distinguish between metal fatigue and a deliberate cut?"

"Depends on the metal," said McEwan. "Apparently this was aluminum cable rather than steel, and aluminum's more susceptible to failure. And, according to the tech, stress corrosion failure can occur without any visible warning signs."

"So lowering the statue of Augustus was the final straw—so to speak."

McEwan's lips thinned as he mashed them together. "Yeah."

I thought rapidly. Dylan Luneau was off the hook for Victor's murder—and so was George. And all of us. And if Victor hadn't been murdered, then there was probably no connection between his death and the missing Celtic artifacts! "So, where does that leave us?"

"In deep shit. No victim, no murderer—no case. My Captain will have a fit that we've devoted so many resources to this investigation." He surged out of his seat, abandoning his half-drunk coffee on the café table. "I'm supposed to be solving homicides, not chasing missing artifacts!" He lunged towards the door and then turned around. "Lisa, don't tell the other staff about this development right away, okay?"

"But why not?"

McEwan shrugged his massive shoulders. "My gut tells me that, despite the lack of evidence, everything that has happened in this nutty museum is connected. My boss may want to assign the artifact thefts to someone else and I'll need time to convince him otherwise."

"Okay, I'll play it your way."

The door swished shut as he left the café.

I stayed put, determined to finish my coffee before I returned to my unanswered emails and messy desk across the street. I wrapped my hands around the warm mug and gazed at a photograph of the Boston Red Sox in last year's playoffs as my brain ticked over.

No mystery over Victor's death. What a lot of misplaced suspicion and mental energy trying to figure out who'd done it!

On the other hand, we still had a series of unsolved thefts of Celtic artifacts. Who was the thief?

Presumably, the thief had connections in the art underworld. We'd filed a report on the Bryn Mawr Torque with the International Council of Museums—they maintained the "List Rouge" of stolen items on the Internet. We didn't expect to see results any time soon.

I didn't have the resources to trace how artifacts moved between Boston, North America, and Europe, but maybe I could help the police figure out how the stuff was getting out of the museum. I'd have to carve out some time to visit the basement, with or without Sara Browning. Soon.

Time to go. I put my mug in the bin near the door and left the café. A glance at a curbside flower island revealed yellow daffodils, just on the verge of blooming. My thoughts digressed to summer and the research trip I hoped to take to Columbia University in New York City. Wait a minute, I should have heard about the travel grant for that trip by now! With everything happening at once, it had completely slipped my mind.

I strode back to my office, shed my coat, and groped for the campus phone book.

"Is that the Scholar's Travel Fund? I'd like to check on my recent application for a Summer Research Grant."

The clerk put me on hold while she checked the database. "I'm sorry, but that grant was withdrawn."

"*What?* But I didn't withdraw it!"

"It says here Dr. Albrecht canceled the application a few days ago."

Shit. I took a deep breath. "That's a mistake, I filed that grant and I certainly didn't want it to be canceled. How can I reinstate it?"

"Sorry. The panel met yesterday, and their funding decisions are final."

My stomach clenching, I replaced the phone and glared at it. Dismally, I remembered that Val countersigned all grant applications that came from museum staff. So that was Val's revenge for humiliating her at the Opening—hitting me where it would hurt most, and removing any chance for a break from routine over the summer. That miserable, rotten bitch.

Brring. "Hello?"

"Lisa, it's David Saltonstall. Could you come down to my office for a few minutes?"

Wondering what was going on now, I said I'd be right there.

As I sped down the stairs to the second floor to Dean's office, a tide of recklessness rolled over me.

He's going to hear about what Val did to me if it's the last thing I do.

~ * ~

"What's Lisa doing here, Dave? I thought you and I were having a private conversation." Valerie Albrecht, looking sleek and dangerous, was already seated at the Dean's table when I entered the room.

"It's *David*," said Saltonstall, pulling out a chair for me. He had a steely glint in his eye that I'd rarely seen before. "I've never liked the nickname Dave. And Lisa needs to be here, because what we're talking about is your performance, Val."

Val's face transformed from its usual cream-fed cat look to a mask of rage. "Then I insist that Lisa Donahue leave at once!"

"She stays. Now, I've just had a phone conversation with Greg Wagner in Anthropology. He told me you were impossible to work with and that he had to withdraw his offer to curate the new exhibit on African initiation customs."

"That's ridiculous, the man is over-reacting. What really happened is—"

To my astonishment, the Dean cut Val off.

"You have also alienated three of our major donors to both the museum and the College of Liberal Arts and Sciences. Each one of them has called me to complain how you rode rough-shod over their perfectly reasonable requests to name galleries or exhibit spaces after them—"

Val sprang to her feet. "I don't have to take this!"

"Sit down, Valerie. As if that weren't enough, I've been checking with your staff and I understand you have undermined them in various ways, preventing them from completing assignments that your predecessor gave them. And Lisa here has borne the brunt of your attempts to divert blame from yourself, especially in her dealings with the architects for the new building..." Saltonstall glanced at me and apparently noticed my parted lips. "You have something to say, Lisa?"

I nodded and glowered at Val. "Val, I called the Scholar's Travel fund to check on my summer research grant. I just found out you canceled my application."

"It was just a scam you cooked up to get yourself out of work and grab a trip to New York—"

"Balderdash! The proposed trip was for legitimate research on our Egyptian collection. That research would have benefited the entire museum—it wasn't a vacation!"

Val tried again, lowering her voice and directing her considerable charm on the Dean. "Dave—David—there's been a big mistake here..." Her voice trailed off.

"You're right, Valerie, I made a big mistake. I hired you when I had a perfectly competent Interim Director who could step up into the permanent position." He turned to me. "Dr. Donahue, are you ready to resume the Director's position, this time for good?"

Be careful what you wish for... you may get it.

I teetered on the narrow ridge between past and future. On one side, I saw my curator duties receding into the distance. On the other side, I saw new vistas of change and challenge.

"Yes," I said with a big smile.

Val exploded. "David, you can't do this to me!"

"Yes, Valerie, I can. You're fired. You have two days to clean out your personal files and turn in your keys."

There was a ghastly pause as Valerie Albrecht lurched to her feet. A pulse beat at her temple, and her lips looked like she'd chewed off her lipstick. "David Saltonstall, you'll regret this. I still have friends in high places. As for you, young lady... watch your back."

The air whooshed out of me as the door closed behind Val. I looked at Dean Saltonstall. "I'm in a state of shock. I can hardly believe that just happened."

A rare smile bloomed on the Dean's face. "I can't believe she didn't slug me in the face. *Not* a nice woman. I should have asked more questions about that overly enthusiastic recommendation from Philadelphia..."

"Oh?" I tried not to sound too eager. This must be the explanation of how Val had been hired so quickly.

"Never mind."

Darn.

He shifted back his chair and stood, stretching. "Well, Lisa, you're in charge now. I wonder what the reactions of your staff will be to this news?"

"Mixed, I'm sure." Little bats of unease swooped in my stomach as I thought of the volatile emotions displayed in the past by Ellen, Dylan, Susie, and Nancy. "A couple of younger staff members were hoping Val would help them get ahead. They may be dismayed at having me back as boss. Um—how long to you think it will take to process my new appointment?"

"I'll get my secretary right on it. Don't worry, Lisa, I won't let this one get screwed up again. Go deal with the fallout, and give me a call in a couple of days and let me know how it's going, okay?" He reached for the phone.

I sensed relief coursing through him, and a little something else, a distinct sloughing off of responsibility. He'd just handed me a big new job on a platter—but that didn't mean he was going to help me do it. Saltonstall's mantra was divide and delegate; so for me, it was pretty much sink or swim.

Put not your trust in Deans.

Twenty-two

Same day, afternoon

After a quick foray for a ham sandwich at a café across Commonwealth Avenue, I phoned my better half.

"James, guess what? I've been promoted."

"Don't tell me someone's finally dropped a statue on Valerie!"

I smiled into the phone. "No. Several people wanted to, but that's not what happened. Val pissed off a professor and several major donors. And the Dean has been keeping tabs on what's been happening with the staff. He fired Val about half an hour ago."

"The guy has some sense, after all. So you're Director again?"

"Looks that way. And Saltonstall says the appointment will be permanent this time." I waited gleefully for his congratulations.

James was silent a little too long.

"Aren't you pleased? James?"

"Sure I am. It's just that—oh, hell, it's a great step for you Lisa. We'll celebrate this weekend, okay? Charlie Sloan's calling me, I've got to go."

I said goodbye and hung up, brow furrowed. What was going on with James? Probably he realized the promotion would mean more late hours for me and less time with him and the kids. That meant that we needed—

"Lisa! I just heard Val's been fired!" Ellen bounded into the office, her blue eyes snapping with excitement. "She's banging around in her office, swearing herself blue, and—"

"How'd you find out so fast?"

"Susie, of course. Someone in the Dean's office just called her. Lisa, it's fantastic! Now you're the Director. Everything will go back to the way it used to be."

Fat chance. Nothing would ever be the same—we'd lost Victor, and George. And I'd have to make decisions in my new role that might not please Ellen, or anyone else on the staff. Out loud, I said, "Not quite, Ellen. We'll all have to adjust. What about Tim—does he know yet?"

Magically, Tim and Susie appeared in my doorway.

Susie wore a Cheshire cat grin. "Finally, Val gets her comeuppance! I almost feel sorry for her."

Tim's mouth twisted into a sneer. "I don't. That lady needs to find a new job—preferably one where she works for herself. No one else can stand her."

I seized the opportunity to do a little delegating. I asked Tim to inform the other staff about Val's firing.

After he left, I suggested that Susie and Ellen help me pack up my office so I could move back into the Director's office as soon as Val left. "It's so much larger, and has the perfect table and chairs for small meetings." I gestured helplessly at my piles of folders and stacks of books. "I can scarcely turn around in here."

Susie gave me her most direct stare. "The rest of us will resume our original job roles and responsibilities now that you're in charge, right?"

I knew she meant her former duties as Assistant Director. "In your case and Ellen's, yes," I said. "But I'm not going to do a blanket reversal of everything Val set up until I've had time to think about it—and meet with each of you."

Satisfied, Susie nodded.

Ellen said, "Let me make a couple of phone calls and I'll be back in a jiffy."

Susie stayed. Her blue eyes darkened as a thought struck her. "How long did the Dean give Val to clear out her stuff?"

"Two days." I paused as the implications hit me. "I think that's too long."

"You bet your booty it's too long," said Susie. "That witch will try to do something—crash the database, steal files, make a copy of the master key—something that will damage our operations after she's gone."

My gut twisted as I realized Susie was right. "What do you suggest?"

"Well, at the law firm where I used to work, someone who'd just been fired was escorted to the door and forced to turn over his keys pronto. And during the meeting with the boss when the firing was announced, someone else threw a few personal items in a box and presented them to the firee at the door. No one was ever allowed to go through files or fiddle with a computer—lawyers deal with too much sensitive personal and financial data."

"Hmm. Well, Dean Saltonstall doesn't—didn't—operate that way." I thought a moment. "I could go back to him and say we have a problem—he certainly understands now that Val can be vindictive—but I'd really like to show him we can manage this situation by ourselves. Think we can?"

"You took duplicates of everything that matters from the Director's office before Val moved in, right?"

"Everything I could think of at the time," I said. "Trouble is, there are stashes of critical files all over the museum because all of our offices are so tiny."

"Tell you what. I have a friend, Todd Sampson, in the Campus Police. What do you say I ask him if he'll meet us at Val's car when she gets ready to leave for the day? Then you'll have the backup authority you need, and we can make sure the only files she takes are personal papers. And we'll do it again tomorrow, and then make sure she turns in her keys. Okay?"

"Okay. Have Todd call me first. I want to make sure we do this by the book. And I'm going to call Dylan right now and have him change the passwords for our Intranet and master database."

"Way to go, Lisa," said Susie with a triumphant grin.

Twenty-three

Tuesday March 4

By mid afternoon the next day, I was stiff all over from sitting at my computer and half crazy from dealing with the deluge of phone calls regarding other problems that had arisen since Val's firing.

I phoned my trusty second-in-command. "Susie? The contractors who are fixing the new floor just called and I have to call them back. Could you check on Val and see what she's up to?"

"Sure thing, boss lady."

I punched in the number for the contractor.

Brian Kenney assured me that he had the solution to the floor-cracking problem in the new museum: a brand-new plastic composite that would bind to anything. He and his men would order the materials immediately. But of course, he couldn't guarantee that everything else would be ready in time for the Grand Opening in June. The electricians had run into a snag with the track lighting.

I hung up and stared out the window. If the exhibits were ready but the floor and the lighting weren't, Dean Saltonstall might still insist we have the Opening on schedule to placate the major museum donors. In that case, we'd use Dylan's back-up plan for positioning the buffet tables to hide the damage. And we could use candles for romantic lighting. Oops, probably not—fire codes would prohibit that. Strategically placed flood lights, then.

My fingers drummed on the windowsill. I really didn't see how we'd be able to finish the move of thousands of artifacts, unpack, and install new exhibits in just a few months—we were short-staffed and overwhelmed already. The Opening would be have to be postponed whether the Dean liked it or not.

Brring.

"Yes?"

"Elise Saltonstall for you on line one."

"Thanks."

Elise was Dean Saltonstall's wife and a pillar of the Museum Friends group. I pushed the "talk" button.

"Elise, how are you?"

"Just fine. I've got wine and cheese organized for the Grand Finale, and six women to bring rum brownies, lemon bars, and tiny cheesecakes..."

I grabbed my yellow pad so I could make notes, but there was no need. Elise Saltonstall was probably the most efficient organizer I'd ever met. I doodled cats fighting while I listened, and I agreed with everything Elise suggested. What a relief to have someone else plan the last event in the old building—especially someone as savvy and competent as Elise. All I had to do was show up. Susie would arrange for student staff to man the tables and make sure at least two of them were over twenty-one so they could open and serve the champagne.

When Elise finally ran out of enthusiasm and news, I remembered that I needed to retrieve donor files from the cabinet in the Greek vase storeroom. Since those files had information critical to my own research, I had no intention of letting Val get away with them. On the way, I could stop for a few minutes in the Greek gallery and check my list of label revisions for the vase exhibit against the artifacts in the cases. Naturally, there hadn't been time to do that since the fiasco of the vase exhibit opening.

Picking up my clipboard and key ring, I crossed the hall to the Temporary Exhibit gallery. The struggle of visitors had dwindled, so I was alone in the public part of the museum. I gazed with satisfaction at the new Swedish cases with their easy-open doors and built-in lighting.

I checked off the labels that were already in place and moved over to the Technology case to determine what still needed fixing.

Wait a minute, that label doesn't go with that *oinochoe*. I stared at the mismatch, dismayed. One of my trusty student assistants had grabbed the wrong vase at the last minute. So that meant the right one was still in the storeroom.

Wheeling around, I walked rapidly back to the hallway and yanked out my key ring. The keys jingled as I flipped through the ones for storerooms 50, 49, 48A. I inserted the correct key in the door of 48A and flipped on the lights.

A chair was overturned and red and black potsherds littered the floor.

Uh-oh.

Then I saw the shoe.

A black Italian leather pump, boasting a two-inch heel. A long, slender leg sheathed in sheer black stockings. Charcoal-gray Armani suit with gold necklace and heavy-linked bracelet.

Valerie Albrecht lay on the floor with one leg twisted at an impossible angle. Her body was between the last case and a large artifact cart piled high with packing materials. More potsherds were scattered around her blood-soaked torso, and file folders were strewn everywhere.

And the smell—that iron-rich odor of freshly spilled blood.

I stood rooted to the floor. As my horrified gaze skittered over the scene, I spotted the murder weapon near Val's shattered skull: a heavy, pointed Greek transport amphora.

New exhibit title: "Potted for Posterity..."

Looks like Greek vases are just as unhealthy for museum directors as Roman statues...

As my addled brain manufactured nonsense, I picked up one of the files and noticed that it was the Sansone folder—containing vital information about one of our major collections. I closed and locked the door with unsteady hands. Groping my way along the hallway like an old woman who'd misplaced her walker, I inched my way back into the museum and the nearest phone at the front desk.

Susie glanced up from her computer. "Lisa! You look awful. What's up?"

"It's Val. She's dead—in the Greek storeroom." I swayed. "I need—I need to sit down."

Susie shot out of her chair and shoved it under my knees just in time. "Put your head down. That's right. Have you called the police yet?"

I mouthed the word "no" and Susie dialed 911. I kept my eyes closed and head down until the sensation of spinning stopped. When I was able to sit up, I found Susie leaning forward with her lips parted.

"The police are on their way. Tell me what happened, for God's sake!"

My thoughts stirred sluggishly. McEwan... he would now have a real murder to solve... Just when he thought he'd been wasting his time at the museum. My boss murdered... no, that wasn't right. I was the boss now. I shuddered as the odor of fresh blood filled my nostrils again.

"Lisa?"

I described the murder scene in as few words as possible. "I can't get my mind around this. I think I'm in shock."

"I'm not," Susie said. "If anyone deserved to be murdered, it was that woman."

"True." I rubbed my temples, hoping the motion would release my brain from its muddy trap. "Just as well McEwan's not listening to us now."

I'd never seen Susie behave so calmly. Normally, Susie would be shrieking and moaning; instead, I was the one on the verge of losing it. Unless—no, that was too horrible to contemplate. Susie wielding the heavy Greek amphora? But she'd have gotten blood all over her raspberry wool suit...

There would be plenty of time to speculate. But the police were on their way; I should try to anticipate McEwan's questions. I felt like the White Rabbit who was always late... who never had enough time...

I fell down the rabbit hole.

~ * ~

A hand shook my shoulder. I raised my head groggily. "Huh?"

Sergeant McEwan loomed over me. Had I fainted? Or even more unlikely, had I dozed a little in the chair while we waited for the police? I knew I was sleep-deprived, but this was abnormal.

"Wake up, Ms. Donahue," he said, not unkindly. "You'll have to show us where the body is."

I staggered to my feet and pushed the curtain of long hair back from my face. At some point, my neat braid had come undone. I probably resembled one of the witches in Macbeth.

"This way."

McEwan, Richards, and Susie followed me through out the public entrance and down the dimly lit hallway. Tim Marsden popped out of his office and followed us.

"What happened?" Tim asked Susie in a low voice.

"Val's dead. Murdered," Susie said with relish.

I heard Tim gasp as I halted in front of the storeroom and handed my keys to McEwan.

The door swung open.

McEwan, who was blocking my view, stopped. Then he turned on me.

"Where's the body?"

"*What?*"

"See for yourself." McEwan moved his bulk to one side.

Same storeroom. Same smashed potsherds and bloodstained bits of paper. A large, elongated bloodstain on the floor. No Valerie.

"I don't believe it!" I cried, peering around foolishly. Tim sidled up beside me, one hand rubbing the fabric of his khaki pants.

"You and me both," said McEwan, his lips twisting. "So I have to ask this, Ms. Donahue: are you sure she was dead?"

"She had a hole in the side of her head." I shivered and wrapped my arms around myself. "I didn't touch her, but I'm sure she was dead!"

"There is a bloodstain on the floor, yes, but scalp wounds can bleed a lot. Perhaps she wasn't as badly injured as you thought."

"But..." I shut my eyes, remembering what I'd seen. When I opened them, I stared right at McEwan and spoke with as much authority as I could muster. "I saw Val with a wound that no one could survive. And judging by the additional blood on her torso, the murderer struck her with the amphora more than once."

"This one?" said McEwan, pointing at the amphora still on the floor.

"Yes. There are others like it in the case on the right, but this one hasn't been moved since I was last in the room."

McEwan crouched over it. "If this was the weapon, then it should have blood and hair on it. Yeah, I see a couple of dark brown hairs and some staining." He focused on the bloodstain on the floor. "It does look like she either dragged herself or was dragged. And if she was dragged..." He rose and strode out into the hallway again. "Then this elevator is very conveniently placed for moving a body."

He lowered his graying dark eyebrows and fixed his gaze on me again. "How long has it been since the time you found Val and when we got here?"

"I—I'm not sure. I was very wobbly after finding her..." I leaned against the wall. "I still am." Pain pulsed in my brain. It was so intense that I though I might throw up. And my vision flickered; I saw colored lights out of the corners of my eyes... murder-induced migraine symptoms?

"She passed out briefly in my chair," said Susie, her eyes huge. "But say, five minutes for her to make her way to my desk and tell me what had happened. Then I telephoned, and you guys showed up in another twelve minutes or so."

"So the body was left alone for what? Twenty minutes?" Tim muttered.

McEwan slapped the wall next to the elevator. "Plenty of time to move it out of the building!" He pulled out his radio and made quick call. "Okay, we'll tape off this storeroom until we find Valerie Albrecht. But I can't process this as a murder scene until we have a body!"

The elevator opened, and several crime scene techs emerged, bearing equipment. McEwan explained that there was no body yet and asked them to stand by. Scowling, he turned back to us.

"Ms. Blake, can you get me Dr. Albrecht's home phone number, just in case she's still alive and managed to go home? And do either of you have a floor plan of this goddamn labyrinth? The whole building, I mean?"

The small part of me that was still functioning understood his frustration with Wigglesworth Hall's multiple levels and oddly placed staircases. "I've never seen one," I said.

"Me neither," Susie said. "The museum uses only a fraction of the building—most of the third and fourth floors, plus maybe five storerooms in the basement. Anthropology, Sociology, and the administration for the College of Liberal Arts and Sciences occupy the rest. Maybe the LAS office has a copy of the floor plan, but Operations and Maintenance is more likely."

McEwan grimaced. "Dammit, I don't have enough manpower to locate a plan and then to search five floors of this joint! Well, we've got to go through our routines. First, we find Albrecht, dead or alive. Then, if she's really dead, we'll have to interview everyone again. Oh, and I need a list of everyone who had keys to this storeroom."

"I can get you a list, Sergeant. And I'll call O&M to get a floor plan." Susie departed, heels clicking on the hard floor. Tim, his face expressionless, followed her.

McEwan steered me back to my office and shoved me gently into a chair. I sagged, allowing my thighs to merge with the chair seat as I listened to McEwan call his captain and Detective Richards. God, I felt awful.

"Right. Lisa—Ms. Donahue—I might as well collect some information now, even though we haven't found your boss. What kind of relationship did you have with Miss Albrecht?"

"Doctor Albrecht," I corrected automatically. The dizziness receded and I sat up straighter. "It was a terrible relationship. But I defy you to find anyone in this museum who actually liked her."

McEwan's dark eyebrows quirked. "This doesn't sound like you. You actually sound cynical."

"Ha-ha. Valerie Albrecht would try anyone's patience. Dylan Luneau and Nancy Phelan would probably give you a different perspective, but Ellen and I have known Val the longest. Here's what's happened recently..." I described my exhibit travails and the fiasco with Ellen's grant.

"So the boss scrapped your vase exhibit?"

"Yes, but she pulls that on everyone—any project has to be dissected and reshaped at the last possible minute so she can feel she's put her mark on it. But she's not—"

He interrupted me. "You'd put many hours and weeks into your work and she tore it to pieces."

"True. I didn't like it, but it wasn't the first time."

McEwan's eyebrows lowered into a straight, hard line. "So you had a powerful motive to injure or kill her."

"Oh, good grief! I hated her management style, I despised her personally, but I did not attack her! And, as I was trying to tell you, she's not my boss anymore."

"Yeah, she's dead or injured."

"No, I mean Dean Saltonstall fired Val yesterday and offered me the Director's position while she was in his office with me. I said yes."

"Interesting. Why did he fire her?"

"Val made several important donors and an Anthropology professor very unhappy." I explained the implications of this for financing the new building and mounting new exhibits.

McEwan's restless gaze darted around the room as he took this in. Then he refocused on my face. "Huh. So, what happened immediately after the scene in Saltonstall's office?"

I told him about the visits of other staff members and their reactions to the news of Val's firing. "Then, Susie suggested we should watch our backs because Val was vindictive enough to steal important files—"

"Which gives you another motive for offing her so she couldn't undermine your new position."

"I told you, I didn't kill her! I'd just achieved some job security—why would I kill Val right after the Dean promoted me to the position of permanent Director? You need to look elsewhere for your prime suspect."

"I'd love to, but I have to eliminate you first. You say someone bashed your boss on the head, but there's no body and no evidence."

I glared at him. "Well, I can't help that. You'll just have to believe me until her body shows up and you've interviewed the others. You'll see, almost everyone had a motive for killing Val. And why are you focusing on me, anyway? I've been a good ally to you in the past."

McEwan wouldn't budge. "Ms. Donahue," he said stiffly. "Just because we've worked successfully together in the past does not mean I can exempt you from suspicion now. Assuming there has actually been a murder, you had opportunity and motive. You even had means—all those heavy Greek vases close to hand."

"God dammit, I wouldn't be crazy enough to murder someone in broad daylight! And if I were, I certainly wouldn't waste a valuable Greek vase on the likes of Valerie Albrecht!"

"Cool it, Lisa. Most people use whatever weapon's nearby if they're angry enough. Besides—"

McEwan's cell phone rang. "Stick around—I have to answer this."

Rage revved me up. Apparently, anger—and the adrenaline it produced—was an effective cure for dizziness. Barely resisting the urge to stamp like a little girl, I left my office and marched toward the lounge.

As I walked further away from McEwan, my footsteps slowed and my anger chilled. Little, slimy strands of fear wrapped themselves around my heart; I could hardly breathe.

It doesn't matter that the body's disappeared, or that killing Val makes no sense. He thinks I did it.

Twenty-four

Same day, evening

James came home a little early, expecting to find the house empty.

He dumped his briefcase on the hall table, riffled through the mail, and then lifted his head.

Small snuffling sounds came from the living room. Oreo, with a catnip mouse? He walked through the pocket doors and discovered a seriously sodden wife: Lisa, wrapped in a blanket, sat on the edge of the couch and hovered over a box of Kleenex.

"Honey? What's wrong?"

"*Everything!*"

Uh-oh. James was an experienced enough husband to realize now was not the time for questions. Instead, he sat down next to Lisa and rubbed her back until the sobs slowed to a trickle. "Now tell me."

She groped in her pocket for some Kleenex and blew her nose. "Val was murdered today. I found her body in the Greek storeroom. But then I went to get help and the body disappeared."

"*What* did you say?" His breath snagged.

"Someone removed the body during the fifteen minutes or so that I was gone."

"How bizarre. Why would a murderer do that? Wouldn't someone who'd just killed a person run away?"

Lisa stared at him. "You know, no one else has asked those questions. Why, indeed. McEwan was entirely focused on 'where,' as in 'where's the body?'"

"That's understandable." James wrapped an arm around Lisa.

"The worst part is that, this time, McEwan suspects me of harming Val—and/or hiding the body."

"Really? He never struck me as stupid."

Lisa shrugged. "Maybe not. Maybe he was just being gruff with me—but he clearly wanted me to know that no one is exempt from suspicion." Her blond eyelashes shimmered with tears. "I'm afraid I didn't behave very well."

"You'd had a shock."

"Yes, you could say that..." she paused. "I feel like such a shit. I didn't do it, but I certainly hated that woman enough to have done it."

"There's a big gap between feeling and action. Most people feel like murdering someone occasionally; very few actually do it."

"Another thing. I've never been *glad* someone was dead before. What does that say about me?"

"Only that you're human. Val was a truly poisonous personality—you said so yourself, more than once."

They sat huddled together, trying to draw strength from each other. James realized it must be almost time to pick up Emma and Sam.

Lisa stirred. "James, do you think McEwan will—"

The phone rang. James answered it and held it out to her, mouthing, "speak of the devil."

He stepped back to give her space, but McEwan's voice was so loud that he could hear every word.

"Why did you go home? I didn't say you could leave the building."

"You didn't tell me I couldn't."

"Fine. First thing tomorrow—eight am—we continue your interview." *Click.*

"Jeez!" Lisa stared at the phone as if it were a viper.

"He's not usually so rude, is he?" asked James.

"No." Her shoulders drooped.

James tried to comfort her. "Look, Lisa, McEwan's on the hot seat. Two deaths in a matter of weeks. And, as you told me last night, he's just found out that one of the deaths was accidental, not homicide."

Lisa nodded. "And he told me his boss is going to think he's been wasting his time at the museum." She looked at her watch. "Time to go get the kids. Shall we drive over together?"

~ * ~

Over dinner—macaroni with celery, onion, and three kinds of cheese—we'd talked about everything except the museum and Val's murder.

Later, I tucked in Emma.

"Mommy, are you upset?"

I sighed. "Yes, sweetie, I am. Things aren't going so well at work." I felt guilty at making the understatement of the century, but Emma was only nine.

"Dad said your boss died," Emma said sleepily.

Oh. James must have told her when he was supervising baths. "That's right, sweetheart."

"I'm sorry, Mommy." Her eyes were already closing.

"We'll talk about it some more tomorrow, okay?"

I kissed her soft forehead and tiptoed out of the room.

Trust James to give Sam and Emma the straight scoop. He believed parents should be very direct with their children—just don't give them any more information than they can handle. I agreed with him—I'd just been too exhausted to deal with the issue.

Downstairs, the house was quiet except for the hum of the refrigerator.

I poured another glass of white wine and collapsed onto the chenille-covered futon. I looked at my wonderful, understanding husband, who sprawled on the other couch with his laptop. He hated being interrupted when he was writing something, but it was now or never. "James, now's not the best time, but it's probably the only time today. Can we talk about Sam?"

James sighed and continued tapping on his keyboard. "I thought we'd been over this ground before. He's just adjusting to our new situation—it will pass."

"Please, James. Look at me—I need your full attention."

He fixed me with a chilly green stare and removed his hands from the keyboard. "I'm listening."

I gripped my wine glass and gathered my courage. "Missing almost two weeks of school isn't normal. Sam has no physical symptoms except vague tummy pains, and those only appear right before he's supposed to go to school. Then, according to our babysitter, he's fine as soon as the rest of us leave the house and the threat of school is removed. Doesn't that sound psychological to you?"

James jumped up and started pacing the room.

"Lisa, I think you're making too much out of this. I've talked to him, several times, and he always says things at school are fine."

Placing my glass on the coffee table, I stood and gripped the back of the futon with both hands. "James, you're a great dad, but I've heard you talk to Sam. You ask leading questions, like 'everything at school going okay?' and then don't give him much time to respond. I think it has something to do with his friends..."

"You think! When did you become such an expert on my son?"

"James!" Tears welled up in my eyes. We were fighting; we never fought. "I spend a lot of time with him in the late afternoons, when you're at the hospital."

"That's right, blame it on my new job! And I spend time with both kids when you're late at the museum!" He gazed back at me, his expression hurt and mystified. "Look, hon, I can't take anymore right now. I'm going for a walk."

He grabbed his leather jacket off the hook and hustled out the back door.

I felt like I'd been kicked in the stomach.

Time to resurrect the Stressometer: add a spike of fifty degrees for finding your second boss (in one semester) killed; add at least twenty degrees for fighting with your husband.

I crossed to the sink, hoping that stacking the dishwasher would calm my nerves. Four plates made it safely onto the racks, but the first glass I picked up slid out of my hands and smashed to slivers on the tiled floor.

I gave up on the dishes. I slumped into a chair and laid my head over my crossed arms on the table.

An old verse written by a junior high school friend tolled in my brain:

"Damn, damn, damn
Cod liver and Spam
Cold fish and salt ham
Damn, damn, damn, damn!"

Twenty-five

Wednesday, March 5

Thursday morning dawned bleak and chilly. I stumbled out to the kitchen in furry slippers and my oldest pink-and-white toweling bathrobe. I couldn't remember when James had crept into bed beside me, but the grittiness of my eyes and the dull thudding in my head told me that whatever sleep I'd managed wasn't enough.

"Mom, did you get any more Honeynut Cheerios?" said Emma, plopping herself onto a chair and hitching herself closer to the breakfast table.

"I'm sorry, sweetie, I forgot yesterday—"

"But you promised!" she whined.

"I'll get some today. We've still got cornflakes." I put the box and a bowl in front of her and retrieved milk from the fridge.

James, polite but distant, hid behind the morning paper. Sam stayed in bed, preferring to have breakfast when the babysitter came and the rest of us were out of the way.

Realizing there would be no reconciliation with James until at least that evening when we could talk privately, I lost my appetite. I inhaled three cups of black coffee and forced myself to down a few spoonfuls of instant oatmeal.

After dropping off Emma and parking my car in the museum's lot, I entered Wigglesworth Hall by the back stairs. I hoped to avoid the police; I'd see McEwan soon enough. I wanted to stop in my office, drop off my briefcase, and check for phone messages before being interrogated. I crossed quickly through the Asian and American galleries.

As I unlocked my door, a little voice in my head said, "Well, at least you won't have to update the exhibit labels. Val doesn't care any more."

And do you care that she's dead?

My emotions were so muddled that my insides felt like scrambled eggs. Sorrow, relief, confusion, and fear chased each other through me like the vivid expressions flitting across my daughter's face.

I needed a task that would distract me but not take too much brainpower. Maybe sorting piles of paper would fit the bill while I waited for McEwan to show up, and Saltonstall to return my call.

I'd placed the call before leaving home, figuring the Dean would appreciate a full account of Val's attack and disappearance from me—rather than from the media—at the earliest possible moment. Action of any kind made me feel more in control, but I worried about how Saltonstall would react to Val's death and the negative publicity that was sure to follow.

And what would McEwan say? What if he insisted I was really a suspect and had no business running the museum? But surely, when he completed all his interviews, he'd realize other staff members had just as much opportunity and motive to kill Val as I did.

Fear gurgled through my blood vessels as I moved a stack of folders from chair to file cabinet. My brain finally absorbed what my gut had known for weeks: that someone on the museum staff was capable of violence and murder. But how ironic that the metals report had downgraded Victor's death from murder to accident just before the second body—this time, definitely a murdered one—cropped up.

A rustle of cloth made me look up from my file sorting. McEwan and Richards loomed in my doorway. "There you are, Ms. Donahue," McEwan said, sounding very stiff and formal.

Uh-oh. Just what I needed in my life—another surly, over-sensitive guy. "Have you found the body yet?"

"No," McEwan said with obvious disgust. "University Police have provided a floor plan. They'll help us check every room in this building, but it will still take hours. Now, I'd like to go over your account of yesterday again."

"Fire away." I removed leaning towers of papers from my two chairs and gestured for them to sit down.

Richards took notes as McEwan took me over the previous day's events.

"That's clear enough," said McEwan. "Now, what was everyone else doing yesterday when Dr. Albrecht was allegedly attacked?"

I matched the chilliness of his tone. "But I don't know when she was 'attacked'—and neither do you since you don't have a body!"

"Let's assume the incident happened yesterday afternoon between three-thirty and five," he retorted. "So, how about it?"

There it was again, that ambiguous word "incident." I looked at McEwan helplessly. "I don't know. You heard Susie say our museum is divided into sections on three different floors..."

Which you know perfectly well from your investigation of the murders three years ago.

"...on any given work day, staff are all over the place, and with the move going on..."

"All right, I get the picture. Did anyone visit you, call you up during that time?"

"There were several calls—one from the architect, another from the Personnel Office. Oh, yeah—I talked to Ellen Perkins around four."

"Ah. That fits with what Ms. Perkins said." McEwan scribbled something in his notebook.

So Ellen had mentioned that phone call. Good—now I had an alibi worth about five minutes.

The phone rang; I picked it up.

"Yes, this is Lisa Donahue. Oh, hello, David... Yes, I agree... actually, could I call you back in a few minutes? The police are with me right now... right. Bye."

I replaced the phone and found McEwan's gaze on my face. "So what did the good Dean want?"

"He was returning my call. I left him a message this morning; I wanted to give him my version of events."

"Lucky I talked to him yesterday afternoon."

"It's my job to keep him informed! Don't forget, a dead staff member is a giant PR problem from his point of view."

"A bit premature, aren't you? Dr. Albrecht might not be dead."

I bit off my words. "No one could have survived that head wound. I *saw* it."

"So you say. We need to see her dead body."

I exploded. "Jeez! What about assuming that I'm telling you the truth, and that I'm innocent until proven guilty?"

McEwan eyed me without even a hint of a smile. "Guilty—or innocent—of what, exactly? Murder, assault, hiding evidence, or all three? Until I know what I'm dealing with, all bets are off." McEwan hoisted himself out of his chair, motioned to Richards, and left the room.

I was sorely tempted to throw a phone book at McEwan's back. Normally, he was the soul of courtesy. Either he'd gotten out of bed on the wrong side today, or he had an ulcer. Or, as James had guessed, he was in a really tough spot because his first murder case had evaporated and a dead body had been mislaid. Still, he didn't have to take it out on me.

Well, since McEwan was acting like a jerk, I had no intention of sharing all my theories and activities. If the police priority was finding Val's body, then mine was finding the missing artifacts. And if I should just happen to find the body before the police, then McEwan would have to change his tune.

Time to find Sara Browning and do a little underground exploration.

~ * ~

"Sara? Have you got time now to show me around the basement?"

"Sure," said the younger woman. Sara shuffled her papers together. "Let's go see if Dylan's keys are in his drawer."

They weren't. And Dylan's office was a shambles; every surface was covered with computer printouts and lists of artifacts related to the move. That meant Dylan had his key ring on him. But as Director again, I was entitled to a master key for every room the museum owned. Crap, I couldn't get them now—I'd have to cross campus and fill out forms at Facilities Management before I could obtain a set. No, wait a minute, what had happened to Val's keys?

I couldn't remember seeing Val's key ring dangling from her belt when I discovered the body. So, that meant that someone besides the police had them.

"Never mind," I said to Sara. "Just give me a tour of the accessible parts of the basement." I looked at my watch. "We've got about half an hour, then I have to pick up Emma. It's one of her 'early out' days."

The elevator dropped us in a dimly lit, gloomy subterranean world. Old pipes, probably asbestos-coated, ran up corners and along ceilings, and countless locked doors lined the corridors. Elderly computer monitors, rejected office furniture, and miscellaneous boxes completed the décor.

What a fire hazard. "Can you believe this?" I asked Sara.

"Looks like this is the dumping ground for the entire University." Sara opened a door I almost missed because I was so busy speculating which department owned which rooms. "Here's the tunnel Brian showed me. It goes all the way to the dorm next to his, halfway across campus."

"Great way to avoid traffic in the Quad between classes," I observed, remembering how many times I'd almost been hit by students zooming along on bicycles.

Sara's brown eyes widened. "Except you never know who might be down here." She wrapped her arms around her slender torso. "I definitely wouldn't use it alone, or at night. And not with people getting murdered in the vicinity."

As we walked the halls, I compared the scene with the lower levels of James' hospital. The hallway to the morgue was comparatively well lit, with a clean floor, no clutter, and rooms on either side that were obviously in active use.

In sharp contrast, this labyrinth was spooky, poorly maintained, and dimly lit. Dusty and derelict stuff lay everywhere, and I smelled mouse droppings and mold. How could I possibly guess the functions of the locked rooms? Not offices, surely. Maybe storage for yet more equipment? For which departments? I had the distinct feeling that hardly any folks came down here, and that if they did, their business must be suspect.

Glancing at my watch, I realized it was getting late and we'd have to turn back. As we approached the junction of the tunnel and the basement under Wigglesworth, I saw a thin form ahead of us, wheeling what looked like a packing crate on a museum cart. He was wearing the uniform and cap of and O&M guy, but something about his gait was familiar.

"Hey! Wait up a minute!" I yelled, breaking into a trot.

The thin man glanced behind him briefly, then put on a burst of speed and rounded the corner before us. As Sara caught up with me, I heard the whine of the elevator going up.

"Damn!" I said. "I really wanted to see who that was."

"I think it was Dylan's friend, but I'm not sure," said Sara. "He was a little too far away."

With a jolt, I realized I had two unpleasant tasks ahead of me. I had to assert my authority with Dylan—always an uncomfortable process since he resented me—and make sure he wasn't hiring people behind my back. Then, I must tell McEwan about the tunnels between the buildings in case the University Police hadn't already done so. In his current prickly mood, he'd think I was either trying to tell him how to do his job or I was withholding information. Either way, he'd bite my head off.

Twenty-six

Friday, March 7

Ellen felt relief when, two days after Val's murder, Lisa called a staff meeting.

It was time for all of them—the staff members who were alive and functioning—to regroup. Ellen observed her colleagues as they shuffled into the meeting room, which also doubled as a library. Two battered wooden tables had been shoved together so the configuration resembled a conference room. The seating was eclectic: padded, swivel chairs, straight-backed wooden chairs, and a couple of metal folding chairs.

Ellen supposed she should feel grateful that she was physically intact, but she was bleary-eyed and emotionally battered after another fight with Dylan.

She watched her best friend in action. Lisa exuded fatigue, like the rest of them, but she looked like she was in charge. As if she'd suddenly grown into the position. Not like her first stint as Interim Director, when she was still groping for the right mixture of authority and sympathy in her voice and attitude. Now, suddenly, she had arrived. And Ellen saw the price it had cost Lisa: a slightly leaner cast of face, a couple of extra fine lines around her eyes. Part of her rejoiced; Lisa deserved to be their permanent Director. The other part of her was pissed that Lisa had been right about Dylan.

The dude in question strolled into the room and took a chair as far away from Ellen as possible.

Ellen regarded Dylan Luneau, who showed no signs of recent emotional trauma, with a jaundiced eye. He was an inconsiderate, juvenile slob. And he was chronically unfaithful. But he cooked divinely, he loved going out dancing, and he was great in bed...

Lisa opened the meeting. "Thanks for coming, everyone. I know we're all stretched to our limits, but I wanted to get us together again. We need to reevaluate, reorganize, and try to get past this, um, 'incident' with Val—"

Someone snickered.

Lisa responded with a wry smile. "Yeah, I know— 'incident' is hardly the right word for a physical assault ending in a death, but it's how the police refer to it. You all know that I'm calling it a murder because I saw the body before it disappeared."

"*We* know it was murder. But the police, understandably, want to see some evidence before they believe Lisa," Ellen said. She was pretty sure the rest of the staff accepted Lisa's version, but she wanted to establish that now.

"If McEwan knew Val the way we did, he wouldn't doubt there'd been a murder, body or no body," Susie said.

"You can say that again," Tim Marsden said.

Ouch, thought Ellen. I can't wait to hear his story! Out loud she said, "That woman was a disaster as a Director. If the rest of you had seen what she did to my grant—" A warning glance from Lisa stopped her.

"Let's not get bogged down in Val stories. We still have a museum to run, a lot of artifacts to move, and a new building to furnish," said Lisa. "Now, McEwan and his team will continue to slow us down until they finish their investigation, but we have to keep our sights on the Grand Opening in June. But before we talk about that, we have to confront one thing."

Ellen saw Lisa's chest expand as she took a deep breath. *Now we get to it.*

"I can't share everything Sergeant McEwan has told me, because he hasn't given me permission to do so.."

Dylan adjusted his position so his chair screeched. He avoided Ellen's probing gaze. Stupid bastard, thought Ellen, he's upset that Lisa has the inside track with the police.

Then a pang of loneliness seized her as she admitted to herself what the latest fight with Dylan signaled: incipient breakup. Splitting up the kitchen equipment and CDs, finding a new apartment and moving on. Nursing her emotional wounds for weeks or months before she dared go on a date again.

Lisa was still talking. "But the fact is, Val's murder was committed by someone who had access to that storeroom. Someone with a master key."

"I hope you don't mean just museum staff!" exploded Dylan. "After all, Operations and Maintenance staff have keys to all our rooms!"

Susie jumped in. "Yes, but what about motive? Don't forget, the people with the motive to kill Val were the ones who worked under her. That's us. The people who knew what a witch she was."

There was a horrid silence while people locked gazes around the table and their bodies shifted uncomfortably.

Nancy, white-faced, added her two cents. "I can't believe any of us would murder someone!" Her brown curls bounced with the force of her feeling.

Ellen knew when to toss the ball back to Lisa. "What you believe or don't believe isn't the issue. Someone who had access to our floor in our building killed Val. It's up to the police to figure out who it was; our job is to cooperate with them and still do our jobs. The thing is, no one should work alone—why don't we pair up, as much as possible?"

"Well said, Ellen," said Lisa. "She's right; that's just what I wanted to propose. Until this case is solved, we all should juggle our schedules so no one is in the museum alone after hours, and as much as possible, two people should work within sight of each other."

Susie protested. "But that's too hard! We've all got different responsibilities—"

Lisa pinned her with a sharp look. "Susie, you of all people should remember that we have a protocol for this." Her gaze swept around the newer staff members. "I'm sure you've all heard about the murders of our registrar and one of our students three years ago—and that was an inside job. This is a different case, but McEwan and Richards are not dummies; they know we all disliked Val, or at least most of us did. And Val had a streak of vindictiveness. She had something on each of us—a knowledge of weakness or vulnerability—that she used to manipulate us."

"You're saying she may have blackmailed someone?" Dylan asked incredulously.

"Yes, but I don't necessarily mean financially. Emotional blackmail was her specialty. But I wouldn't put anything past her. Ellen knows—we both worked under her in Philadelphia."

Ellen nodded, pleased that Lisa was speaking so plainly. "Even Lady Macbeth couldn't compete with Val for deviousness."

"Aw, you gals were just jealous of her. I mean, she was so smart, so attractive—" Dylan said.

Heat flowed up Ellen's chest and face. "Spoken like a man!" she sneered.

Dylan frowned. "Yeah, maybe, but Tim and I *are* the only men here. This place is lousy with females, and everyone knows females fight like cats."

"What do you think, Tim?" Ellen asked, curious to hear what he had to say.

"Val was a terrible advisor," Tim said. "The Head of Art History put her on my committee as a replacement for Victor. Then it was just delay after delay, rewrite after rewrite..." His voice dropped to a low mutter.

"So Tim's reaction to Val had nothing to do with her sex. It was her behavior as an advisor," Ellen said.

But that does give Tim a motive for wanting Valerie Albrecht out of the way...

"Where's Sara?" Lisa said, changing the subject.

"Haven't seen her today," Susie said.

"Did she call in sick?" asked Lisa.

"Nope." Susie's hard blue stare showed what she thought of that.

Nancy blushed. "Maybe she... no, that can't be right."

"You know something, Nancy?" Lisa leaned forward.

"She was upset about something yesterday. I saw her leave early," Nancy said with obvious reluctance.

"I'll call her home number, Lisa, and find out what's going on," Susie said.

"Thanks," Lisa said. "Tell me right away when you locate her. Now, what we really need to talk about is the Grand Opening. I think it will have to be postponed for a couple of months. But before I make that decision—which Dean Saltonstall is not going to like—I want to hear from each of you how far along you are with plans for reinstallation of the exhibits in the new building."

Hurray, something ordinary to discuss instead of murder! Ellen made a couple of suggestions, and then everyone else jumped in with plans for remounting old exhibits and installing three new displays to fill the expanded gallery space.

Lisa took notes and listened.

Dylan summarized. "About three-quarter of the boxes are in place in each new gallery. The cases are all ready, it's just a matter of unpacking and putting artifacts in—"

"Er, there's a bit more to it than that," Nancy said.

"Right," Ellen said. "Like finding and painting all the artifact stands you need, redoing most of the labels, and checking the lighting."

"Well *yeah*," sneered Dylan. "I know what's involved. After all, I am the preparator..."

"Then why don't you act like it?" snapped Susie.

Lisa rapped the table with her clipboard, making everyone jump. "Everything I've heard from other museums trying to do this kind of move indicates we need more time," she said soothingly. "I've been told most estimates are wrong by at least thirty percent. And I think with a police investigation complicating things, we just can't do it. I'm going to recommend we set the date for early September—right at the beginning of the new semester. That gives us the entire summer to get organized. Agreed?"

Sighs of relief all around.

"Okay, I think we're through here. Dylan, could I have a word?"

His expression sullen, he nodded.

"My office, then, in about fifteen minutes."

Most people scattered and went back to their various duties.

Ellen lingered to chat with Lisa. She wanted to discuss Tim's possible motive for killing Val, and ask whether Lisa was going to say anything to McEwan.

But Nancy Phelan forestalled her.

"Lisa, I didn't want to say anything during the meeting, but the reason Sara was upset yesterday was that she had an encounter with Dylan."

"What kind of encounter?" Ellen said in a frosty voice.

"Well, she's got a crush on him, so she follows him around..."

"Good grief!"

"So yesterday Dylan finally blew up at her and told her to do her job and stop bugging him every five minutes."

"So Sara went home early?" asked Lisa.

Nancy hesitated. "I think so. I mean I saw her grab her coat and purse, so I assumed she was leaving the building."

"Ellen, could you call her home number in Duxbury and see if that's where she's hiding out? We sure don't need another staff member disappearing. If we can't locate her quickly, then I have to tell McEwan."

A little chill settled on the back of Ellen's neck.

After all, we still have a murderer around here.

Twenty-seven

Saturday-Monday, March 8-10

The weekend was literally a washout. It rained torrents, the kids were fractious, and James was hardly home. He was on call all of Saturday and then disappeared to play pick-up basketball with some of his buddies on Sunday afternoon.

I didn't complain; I knew the intense exercise and hanging out with neighborhood guys—a mechanic, a law professor, and a hardware store owner—kept him sane. Half the fun of it, James always said, was spending time with people who had nothing to do with medicine.

James and I were back on track—sort of. At least we'd agreed not to disagree any more about Sam, and that both of us would do our best to persuade him to talk.

At the moment, my major concern was how to refrain from clobbering my children. Why did rainy days always bring out the worst in them?

"I'm sick of Monopoly! Besides, you cheat!" Emma bounced on the couch, knocking cushions onto the floor.

"I do not! I'm just better at it than you."

"I won the last game."

"Only because Mom put away the board before we were finished!" Sam pulled Emma's blond hair and they both ran shrieking through the house.

After I broke up the fight and got out the painting supplies for some enforced quiet time, I started the kettle for more coffee. I looked longingly at the bottle of wine on the counter, but it was well before six o'clock. Too early, especially since I was trying to curb my consumption.

While measuring coffee, I recalled the short, awkward conversation I'd had with Dylan in my office after the last staff meeting.

"Dylan, who's the new guy?"

"What new guy?" Dylan asked, lounging on the edge of my desk.

"The one who helped serve at the Opening. I think I also saw him in the basement, moving a packing crate."

"Oh, that's Steve. He works for O&M part-time, and was looking for extra hours. I hired him just before Victor was killed by that damn statue."

"I see. Did you ever file the paperwork with Susie? She didn't seem to know anything about it."

"Ah—I was going to, but things got crazy around here." He avoided my gaze.

Why was Dylan so prickly around me? I would have guessed that he lusted after my job, but his attitude had been exactly the same when I was just a curator. Maybe he sensed how much I disapproved of his relationship with Ellen. Whatever the reason, he behaved as if he didn't need to explain his actions to me. "Look, if someone new is on the staff, I need to know about it—"

"Victor knew about it! He told me to hire extra help, put them on the academic hourly payroll. I can't help it if he didn't inform you!"

The whistling of the kettle put an end to my uncomfortable memories. As I poured boiling water through the coffee filter, I tried to think of ways to manage Dylan so he'd be more cooperative.

~ * ~

By Monday morning, I was thrilled to dump the kids off at school and immerse myself in work. I smiled as I climbed the stairs, remembering my post doc research job after Emma was born. My boss had failed to understand why I heaved a sigh of relief when I arrived at his office and hung up my coat. I'd explained how chaotic it was to get a baby ready for daycare, feed the cat, eat breakfast, pack lunches, and get out the door on time. Inevitably, Emma spit up on my blouse or needed changing a second time, or a phone call delayed us. Then there was the drive through rush hour traffic. Conclusion: the hardest part about working was getting there—the rest was easy.

As I passed along the hallway on the fourth floor, sunshine peeked through the clouds that had blanketed Boston all weekend.

My mind turned to the most pressing problem: we still hadn't located Sara Browning. I wanted to believe that she had fled home to Duxbury for the weekend, but a niggling feeling in my gut told me otherwise. As soon I reached my office, I planned to call Sara's apartment in Cambridge and her parents' home for the third time.

I stopped in the staff room to start a pot of coffee. Dang it, my favorite coffee was almost used up—and I'd bought the last can. Well, caffeine was my drug of choice. I figured if the supply in the building ran out, all the more reason for me to take a break and go to the nearest Starbuck's or Eddie's.

Finally installed in my paper-strewn lair, I made the phone calls and left urgent messages on two answering machines. I'd just opened my email when someone barged through my doorway.

"Lisa," Ellen gasped. "You've got to come with me."

Hearing an odd note in my best friend's voice, I spun my chair around and looked at Ellen. Her face was skim milk pale, and her eyes were huge. "What's wrong, Ellen?"

Ellen grabbed the back of my spare chair as if she needed support. "I'm not sure—or rather I'm pretty sure, but I wish I weren't... Oh, hell, I'm not making any sense."

She cleared her throat and began again. "We have an extra mummy in the Egyptian storeroom. And the body inside the wrappings isn't ancient."

My heart skittered in my chest. Val? It couldn't be; that was the stuff of horror movies. "How did you find it?" I croaked.

"The smell is overpowering—clearly, it's not a competent job of embalming."

I had to ask. "Could it be...Val?"

"I don't know—I couldn't look at it properly." Ellen closed her eyes and took a deep breath. Then she met my gaze. "I think it could be."

"Okay, I guess I'd better see it. Then, if it's what—who—we think it is, we call in the cavalry."

I grabbed my keys and noticed my hand was shaking. Just what I needed: another—or rather, the same—dead body. I glanced at Ellen as we headed for the storeroom. "Are you okay?"

Ellen gave a poor imitation of her signature grin. "I'm walking, I'm talking. I feel sick to my stomach, but I'll live. Whoever's inside that mummy sure won't."

We pounded down the stairs to the third floor and the long, olive green hallway. Our feet sounded loud upon the cracked linoleum floor.

Ellen pulled out her keys and opened the door to 39B. A draft of fetid air, smelling of something unmentionable, engulfed us.

"Whew!" I said. "I see what you mean." I dropped back to let Ellen lead the way between tall, gunmetal gray shelving, stacked to the ceiling with Amratian vases from northern Egypt, trays of Greek potsherds from Oxyrhynchus, papyri in acid-free tissue, sandals, baskets, and mummies.

The Boston University Museum of Archaeology and History owned exactly four human mummies from different periods of Egyptian history. We also had a couple animal mummies—an ibis and a hawk. I'd done several Egyptian exhibits, so I knew two of the human mummies were on display. According to what I remembered from the database, there should be only two more mummies in this storeroom.

There were three.

I covered my mouth and nose with one hand, unconsciously imitating Ellen as we arrived at aisle four, section A, shelf two. I peered incredulously at the long bundle at the level of my chin.

Ever molecule in my body protesting, I dragged over a stool and stepped up so I could see the mummy's full surface.

It was longer than most ancient mummies, and the wrappings were looser. Much looser. And they were the wrong color—off white instead of brown. I saw crisscross bandaging, like many Roman-period mummies, but crudely executed. No gold studs—and no face portrait.

Reaching out to touch the foot area, I made the mistake of uncovering my nose.

The ghastly odor of putrefaction smacked me in the face.

Gagging, I quickly undid a coil of linen.

This mummy still had flesh on its bones. In fact, it had all ten toes, with the nails painted in the shade of red that reminded me of dried blood. Sheer, expensive-looking stockings.

I undid one more length of linen so I could see if the body was fully clothed.

It wore a charcoal-gray suit.

"It's Val," I said, choking back bile.

"'Mad Museum Director Becomes Mummy,'" said Ellen. "Oh, God, I feel sick." She rushed out into the hall.

~ * ~

I sank down onto the floor and propped my head up with hands. When I felt steadier and my stomach stopped gurgling, I pulled out my cell phone and punched in Sergeant McEwan's number.

"McEwan here."

Deep breath. "It's Lisa Donahue at the Museum. We've found the body of Valerie Albrecht."

McEwan's voice was sharp. "Where?"

"In the Egyptian-African storeroom. The thing is..." I gulped air. "...someone wrapped her up as a mummy."

"*What?*"

I took another belly breath. "It looks like someone tried to embalm the body in ancient Egyptian style, but he or she didn't do a very good job."

"So we have a kinky murderer who makes his victims into mummies? *Shit.*"

"Maybe. And there's another thing." I gripped the phone harder. "Sara Browning's missing. We thought she'd skipped work because of a run-in with a colleague, but no one has seen her since midday Friday. I've called her home number—"

"But today is Monday, and it's after ten," McEwan said with a distinct edge to his voice. "Don't you guys have a system in place to keep track of your employees?"

"Sara Browning's a student—an undergraduate with a full class load. She only comes in for a few hours on Monday, Thursday and Friday, so this is actually the first day she's not where she's supposed to be."

"I'll be there in fifteen minutes," McEwan said

I left the storeroom in a hurry.

~ * ~

Ellen and I stood by as McEwan and Richards lifted the mummy that was once Valerie Albrecht.

Ellen, still pale but composed, cleared off a table so the police could place their grisly burden at a level where we could all see it easily.

Gingerly, McEwan poked around with one gloved hand, peeling back the bandages that wrapped Valerie's torso. In addition to the noxious odors of putrefaction, an odd, sweet smell wafted through the room. As his efforts revealed a long slash through the layers of skin and muscle, Richards turned green and stepped away from the table.

"Sir—I can't do this..." He gagged. "I need to go outside for a moment."

Ellen grabbed his arm and kept him upright.

McEwan sighed. "Come back as soon as you can, Richards. Miss Perkins, not a word to anyone about the condition of this body, okay?" Ellen nodded and guided Richards out of the room.

"Okay, what are you seeing, Ms. Donahue?"

Hang on, Lisa.

I told myself to act like a medical examiner, a professional body handler who didn't know the dead person. I noted the relative lack of bleeding around the torso wound compared to the amount of blood there'd been when I'd found Val dead in the storeroom—probably a sign that this cut had been made after death. "I think—it looks to me like the murderer was trying to remove the internal organs."

And, I thought with an inward quiver, that means that the murderer really hated Val. Killing her wasn't enough—the body had to be mutilated, too.

"Explain," said McEwan.

"Well, if the murderer was trying to imitate ancient Egyptian embalming, he'd take out the internal organs that cause decay: the lungs, liver, stomach, and intestines. Sometimes, the Egyptians also removed the brain, through the bone at the back of the nose." I focused on the skull, praying I wouldn't see any evidence of brain removal. Val's skull appeared to be intact, but her eyes were open. I wished someone would close the eyes; the fixed stare of those hazel eyes unnerved me.

"So what did they do with the organs, throw them out?"

"No, they embalmed them separately and either put them in Canopic jars representing the four sons of Horus—like the ones on the shelf, over there—or placed them in linen-wrapped packages and stuffed them back inside the mummy."

"Know anyone on the staff who's really into mummies—besides yourself?"

I met his somber gaze. "No."

McEwan's expression altered slightly. "You sure know a lot about mummies, but I really don't think you're stupid enough to try a stunt like this."

"Thanks a lot. If I ever made one, I'd do a much better job. This is a crappy mummy."

"Oh? What makes a crappy mummy?"

"Well, the bandaging is very clumsy, the brain's still in place, there's no decoration..." I gave him a short description of what a Roman-period mummy should look like. "The Roman-period embalmers took shortcuts. They usually ignored the preservation of tissues and organs in favor of making the outside of the mummy look pretty."

"Hmm," McEwan said, continuing his evaluation of me as a suspect out loud. "You're a mummy expert, and you've been married to a doc for several years, so you've probably acquired some basic medical knowledge by now..."

"You leave James out of this!"

McEwan raised his hands. "Don't worry, lady, he's not involved. You are."

"What I am is a professional who wants to keep her new job. Would I really risk everything by killing my ex-boss and then trying to embalm her?" I was really steamed now.

"Someone did."

I couldn't argue with that.

"But there are other candidates who hated Ms. Albrecht and were at least somewhat familiar with Egyptian mummies."

I brightened. "So I'm off your list of prime suspects?"

McEwan's eyes became black pools of speculation "We'll see. It would help if you had an alibi for both the time of death and whenever the body was mummified. Ms. Albrecht died sometime during the last week, but I bet the exact time will be hard to pin down because we didn't find her body right away." McEwan turned to Richards, who'd just reentered the storeroom, and gave him some quick instructions about shifting the body to the medical examiner's office.

"Sergeant?" I said. "I've just thought of something."

"Yeah?"

"There has to be another location—a storeroom or somewhere out of the way—where the embalmer worked. And I bet it's in this building."

"I agree—he had to have a knife at least, and a drop cloth or something, maybe some jars for the organs. Okay, let's write down every single thing you did over the last week, who you talked to, where you were when, and then you can tell me why someone would go to the trouble to make a mummy instead of just making the body disappear. First, though, I think we both need a cup of coffee."

I felt some of the tension drain out of me as McEwan put a large hand under my elbow and steered me towards the elevator.

"And, if you can stand it, I think the medical examiner would like to hear your summary of Egyptian embalming. So we'll stop by the morgue."

"Oh, goody."

Twenty-eight

Same day, afternoon

McEwan didn't believe in paying Starbuck's prices very often, so we stopped at a Bigfoot gas station for carryout containers of rotgut coffee and cheese sandwiches. Then we drove to the city morgue.

On autopilot, I ate a few bites of my sandwich before I realized more food would just make me queasier. I'd never been to the city morgue and wasn't looking forward to the experience. Actually, I'd never visited James' hospital morgue either—only the hallway leading up to it. Once, during my first marriage, I'd thought that maybe a good pathologist's wife should visit her husband's workplace and observe him doing his job, but mature reflection had convinced me that witnessing an autopsy had nothing to do with marital happiness.

McEwan, always a fast walker, strode ahead of me into a large room equipped with stainless steel tables, sinks, and cooler drawers. Just what I expected from all those TV dramas, except that television left out the smells: nasty whiffs of bodily fluids, the sharp tang of bleach, and whatever they used to preserve the organs—formaldehyde?—that were kept for further examination.

The medical examiner straightened up from a half crouch over his autopsy table. Dr. Wilson was a scarecrow, over six feet five and thin enough to actually be stuffed with straw. He eyed me from under bushy gray eyebrows. "I'm Dick Wilson. You the archaeologist I've heard so much about?"

Wondering just what McEwan had said about me, I nodded.

Wilson led us over to the far table, where a long, shrouded shape rested. Without giving me any time to brace myself, he whipped off the drape and revealed the unclad head and torso of Valerie Albrecht.

Val's hair was unbound—it made her look younger than her usual French twist. She had large breasts, hardly sagging at all. Too bad her skin was that awful greenish tint. My reluctant gaze traveled downwards to the long incision in her abdomen. I gulped as acid hit the back of my throat.

"So you think someone was trying to embalm this lady like an ancient Egyptian?" Wilson said.

"That's my theory, yes," I said. "Um, it looks like you haven't started the autopsy."

"Yeah. I wanted to hear what you had to say, first."

I averted my eyes from the corpse and repeated what I'd already told McEwan about removal of the viscera. "The Egyptians believed that the heart was the seat of the soul, not the brain, so the embalmers usually left the heart in place and took the brain out. Or at least, they did that during the height of mummification and when their clients could afford it."

"Bet they took the heart out by accident sometimes," Wilson observed shrewdly, rubbing his gloved hands together.

"You're right, actually. CT scans have shown that embalmers screwed up sometimes."

"How'd they take the brain out?"

I swallowed again. It was one thing reading about organ removal; it was quite another to talk about it in this grisly environment, with a dead body right in front of me. "With a hook—through the bone at the back of the nose."

"The ethmoid bone," nodded Wilson enthusiastically. This guy didn't have a squeamish cell in his body. He reached down and opened the jaws of the corpse so he could peer inside. "Hand me that flashlight, would you?"

McEwan passed the light over to the pathologist.

"Aha! Looks like a crude attempt to get at the brain. Didn't work, though."

Forcing myself to look at Val's face, I asked, "How can you be sure of that before you open the skull?"

"Hole's not big enough. Want me to hold the light so you can see properly?"

"I'll take your word for it." I caught a faint grin from McEwan.

"Okay, what did the Egyptians use to embalm the tissues, after they took the organs out?" Wilson said.

"Well, they used a type of salt—*natron*, from a special location in Egypt—for the desiccating of the entire body, inside and out, and then they used a variety of balms made from pine resins and sometimes bitumen."

"What about honey?"

I frowned. "I can't remember if the Egyptians used honey as a regular thing, but there's something in Herodotus about the Babylonians using honey. And Alexander the Great's mummy was supposed to be covered with honey."

"So was this lady. I had to wash the body before I could even begin to do an autopsy."

Honey. I'd read something recently—no, it was a conversation—about honey and embalming. But my shocked brain wouldn't kick in and pull up the details.

Wilson asked a few more questions and then picked up a long, sharp knife. "Would you like to witness the autopsy?"

My legs wobbled and I gripped the edge of the table. "No... I'd rather not, she was my boss. I knew her... oh, God."

McEwan caught my arms and kept me from sliding down onto the cement floor. "Easy does it! Thanks, Wilson. Fax your report to me as soon as you can, okay? I'm going to remove Ms. Donahue before she faints."

He guided me back through the morgue to the reception area and pushed me into a chair. "Put your head down on your knees."

I complied, feeling like a small child. I breathed hard through my nose until the dizziness faded enough for me to sit up. "Thanks. Once I'd have said I wasn't the fainting type, but I seem to be doing a lot of it lately."

McEwan's dark eyes regarded me steadily. "You're doing fine. Many of my officers go green immediately the first time they visit here. You actually carried on a conversation."

Apparently I was back in McEwan's good graces. "Well, the only thing that kept me upright was talking about mummies. They fascinate me."

McEwan snorted. "Yeah, I've noticed. Quite a macabre subject you've chosen. But then you keep marrying doctors, so I guess you're used to it."

I smiled ruefully. "True. Our dinnertime conversations about X-rays and organs aren't everyone's cup of tea. And my gross-out threshold is pretty high after living with two medical specialists."

"Better you than me. Going back to work? I'll drop you off."

~ * ~

That night I couldn't sleep.

James and I had talked everything over. I'd told him about finding Val-the-Mummy and about nearly fainting in the morgue. Unfortunately, the conversation hadn't calmed me down—my brain raced while my spouse snoozed peacefully beside me. Museum staffers, morgue attendants, and cops paraded behind my closed eyelids. All of them argued with me, refuting every theory I offered. I turned my pillow over for the third time, hoping the coolness from the underside of the pillowcase would lull me back to sleep. As I fought with the covers (quietly, so I wouldn't wake James), my mind played back the finding of Val's body.

Val in her tight gray skirt, covered with blood and potsherds, surrounded by donor files, the artifact cart nearby—wait, had the cart still been there when I'd returned with McEwan? No, it couldn't have been. We'd all crowded into the room next to the body.

Now thoroughly awake, I rolled onto my back and opened my eyes. The dim glow of the nightlight in the master bathroom allowed me to stare at the peeling paint of the ceiling above.

I didn't remember mentioning the cart to McEwan at all. The murderer must have used it to move the body. Probably he'd covered the dead or dying Val with packing materials and then moved everything right across the hall into the elevator—a distance of no more than ten feet.

Feeling hot and queasy, I shoved the layer of blankets down to my waist.

But why move the body at all? James had asked that. The murderer wouldn't move the body except to hide it, meaning he—or she—didn't want it discovered right away...

And then I remembered what McEwan had said:

"...tell me why someone would go to the trouble to make a mummy instead of just making the body disappear..."

I sat up in bed so suddenly that James snorted in his sleep.

Why make a mummy at all? Doing a good job of embalming was time-consuming, messy, and an awfully risky activity for someone who presumably wanted to obscure any connection between himself and the body.

I was looking at the situation the wrong way. We'd all been assuming that Val's murderer and Val's embalmer were the same person. But there was no shortage of people who hated Val.

What if there were two people, one who wanted Val out of the way, and the other who wanted to mutilate her body?

I hunched up into a ball. This was definitely a nightmare—only I was wide awake.

I forced myself to continue my analysis. So, criminal number one bashed Val on the head and left the scene as quickly as possible. Then criminal number two—who just happened to be nearby when I left the storeroom—removed the body and took it somewhere to eviscerate it and make a mummy out of it. Brrr—my back erupted in goose bumps.

I grabbed the extra quilt at the foot of the bed and pulled it around myself. I remembered the connecting door, rarely locked, between the Greek vase storeroom and the Roman storeroom. Had it been closed all the way? I closed my eyes, trying to visualize it. Open or shut, it would have been so easy for a second person to lurk behind that door and wait until I stumbled out into the hallway after finding Val's body.

Good theory. The only trouble with it was that it meant there were two crazy people on the museum staff instead of just one.

Twenty-nine

Tuesday morning, March 11

The reporters lurked in the parking lot, waiting like vultures until I left the safety of my car. As I locked my door, I wished I could dazzle them just by existing, like Princess Diana.

A microphone was thrust near my lips. "Ma'am? Is it true your museum director is now a mummy?"

"No comment," I said, imitating a battering ram in my efforts to move from car to museum entrance without being stopped by a reporter.

"Do you think she was murdered by someone on the museum staff?"

I pressed my lips together and pushed forward with elbows and briefcase.

"Do the police think it's the same guy who killed the last Director, Victor Fitzgerald?"

These reporters didn't know that Victor's death was no longer a murder, but it sure wasn't my job to enlighten them. I turned around right in front of the back door to the museum and faced the mob. "I have a meeting with the

Dean of LAS in a few minutes. Together, we will issue a press release later today. I have nothing to say to you right now."

"But Miss! Can't you tell us whether—"

They crowded around me. My hands shook, but I managed to unlock the heavy metal door, squeeze inside without leaving my briefcase behind, and then slam it in their faces. Jerks. Obviously, there were no other good news stories in the city of Boston this morning!

I climbed the stairs two at a time, my mind busily posing the questions David Saltonstall might ask. The main thing was to give him a complete briefing with nothing held back, so he'd feel he was in the loop and that I was doing my job as Director.

Stopping in my office only long enough to hang up my coat and comb my hair, I grabbed my meeting notebook—the only way I'd found to keep track of everything people told me or asked me to do—and headed for the Dean's office.

"Go right in, Lisa," said the secretary, smiling.

"Thanks, Diane."

She's only smiling because she has no idea what we're talking about.

A weary-looking Saltonstall stood up immediately when I entered the inner sanctum. "Lisa! Do sit down. I appreciate your phone call last night giving me a heads-up on this awful situation."

"I knew the Press would pounce on us first thing, so I wanted you to know immediately."

"And did they? Pounce on you, I mean?" Saltonstall sidled out from behind his desk to sit facing me.

"They sure did. I felt like Princess Diana fending off awkward questions about the royal family. I gave them exactly nothing and told them we'd be making a joint statement later."

A ghost of a smile flitted over Saltonstall's face. Then his eyebrows snapped into a straight line. "Tell me everything that happened yesterday."

I stuck to the facts and left out all my speculations and nightmare visions.

"Lisa, this is a full scale disaster for the Museum—and for the College. If we can hush up the fact that the former Director is now a mummy—"

"Too late. The reporters knew all about it before I said anything today."

"How the hell do they do it?" The Dean shook his head in frustration. "Sometimes I think they have spies in every University building, they get bad news so quickly. Let me think a moment..."

I stared at a row of framed portraits of former Deans—all balding, middle-aged men—on the opposite wall.

"Okay, here's what we do. We tell them Valerie Albrecht's body was found among the mummies in the Egyptian storeroom but deny she was made into a mummy."

"Can we get away with that?"

"I'm sure the police don't want the mummification aspect of the murder revealed until they have someone in custody."

"True. But the staff will talk..."

"You said only Ellen Perkins and Tim Marsden were there with you when the police examined the body. Did you tell anyone else?"

"No, there wasn't time. Besides, Sergeant McEwan made them promise to keep quiet about the attempted embalming..." I bit my lip. "But that means—"

Saltonstall got there before me. "Surely the other staff guessed that Val had been found from all the commotion and police activity. But if they didn't actually see her, who leaked the information about the condition of her body?"

We looked at each other.

"Must have been the guy who made her into a mummy," I said.

"You mean, the murderer."

I hesitated and then nodded. Saltonstall was already having a bad day—he really didn't need to hear my theory that there were two criminals at large instead of one.

Not until I had some solid proof.

I was about to leave when the Dean's phone rang.

"Yes?" It sounded like he was talking to Diane again. "What do they want?... really... oh, hell, I suppose so." He glanced at his watch. "Why don't you tell them we can meet at one o'clock?"

Saltonstall replaced the phone in its cradle and turned a grim expression on me. "We have a problem. Some of the Board members think we should close the museum until both the murders and the thefts of artifacts are solved. At least three of them are coming here at one to discuss it."

I was appalled. "But solving both crimes could take months! And we just changed the date for the Grand

Opening. Don't they realize a closure at this point will delay the opening of the new building even longer?"

The Dean leaned back in his chair. "Apparently, their argument is that the safety of the museum staff—not to mention our more valuable artifacts—is more important than opening on time."

I rubbed my temples. I'd already rescheduled our publicity blitz with the university's News Bureau. And a long closure at this point might mean some of the staff would seek other jobs... Then I had an idea. "If Sergeant McEwan is available, can he come to the meeting?"

"Sure. His presence could be very helpful."

I excused myself and almost ran for the door. I had some urgent phone calls to make.

~ * ~

The College of Liberal Arts and Sciences' boardroom was much more posh than anything inside our museum—either the old boardroom in Wigglesworth Hall one or the new one in the Taylor building. A huge, oval table dwarfed the elegantly upholstered chairs and the walnut credenza in the corner. Framed photographs of past college presidents glared down on us while the genuine Oriental carpet muffled our footsteps.

At one end, Mavis Driscoll, a sixty-something Boston matron with white hair and a mauve wool suit, conferred with "good old boys," Gerald Higgenbottom and Harold Cabot. Cabot was a patent lawyer, tall and beautifully dressed in a tailored navy blue suit. Higgenbottom, a bigwig in the fish-packing industry (formerly "the codfish aristocracy"), presented a sharp contrast with his small, weasel-like face and ill-fitting brown suit. Any deficiencies in appearance, however, were more than compensated for by his background; like the other two, Higgenbottom was a Boston blue-blood, born into money and privilege that went back seven generations.

As I took my seat about halfway down the table, three pairs of eyes regarded me coolly, making me feel like a cat that had just entered a room full of dogs. I pulled out my pad of paper on which I'd jotted down a few arguments for keeping the museum open.

The museum's Board was advisory, meaning its members could propose policies and vote on recommendations, but the final decisions were made by the Director—usually. If the Director disagreed violently with the Board, then the Dean was the final arbiter. If I'd had Victor's experience and clout, I wouldn't be so nervous. However, I was new to my job, relatively young, and not from an old Boston family—the Donahues were Scotch-Irish-German mongrels. No wonder my hands were clammy and a band of tension encased my forehead.

Jeannie Barker, a slight, dark-haired woman who served as a volunteer docent as well as a member of the Board, slid into a seat next to me. Her friendly smile told me even more than her position at the table; she hadn't yet decided what position to take on the closure of the museum.

David Saltonstall and Bruce McEwan entered the room almost simultaneously. David chose a neutral position across from me, not next to any board members, and McEwan surprised me by taking a chair on my left.

"Okay," said the Dean. "As you all know, we have two unsolved murders and a series of thefts from the Museum.

I'd like to hear from the Board first, and then we'll have updates from Dr. Donahue and Sergeant McEwan."

Harold Cabot adjusted his tie and cleared his throat. "Well," he began, "I think it's obvious that both the collections and the staff are in danger as long as the building is open—"

Mavis stuck her oar in. "It's just crazy to let people work up there. There's no security at all. Why, the museum doesn't even have proper guards—just students and occasional staff members, parked at desks in the galleries. Even I could walk off with a valuable artifact."

Cabot fixed Mavis with a cold stare. Clearly, he didn't like being interrupted. "Mavis, that will all be taken care of in the new Taylor building because the budget allows for hiring professional security men. What we have now is a much more serious situation requiring either the closure of the museum or a police presence twenty-four hours a day. Two of our major donors, Mr. and Mrs. Samuel Lowell, couldn't be here today, but I've talked with them on the phone, and they are of the opinion that the museum should be closed until the crimes are solved to protect everyone's interests."

That sounded very proper and lawyerly, I thought sourly. "I appreciate the Lowells' concerns," I said, "but you must understand that the process of moving the entire collection to the new Taylor building is already behind schedule. We're short-staffed and overwhelmed as it is. If we delay the work again, there's no possibility of opening the museum on time—"

"I thought you had already moved the Grand Opening of the new museum to September," Higgenbottom said, peering at me as if I were some new species of insect.

"Yes, that was in response to losing Victor and George. We have over forty-five thousand artifacts, not to mention those enormous statues, to pack, move, and unpack with a permanent staff of six plus assorted undergrad students. Then, we have to mount several new exhibits and install new labels over the summer."

Jeannie said, "Surely Mr. and Mrs. Lowell would change their minds if they heard how much still has to be done. I know I thought the move was almost completed."

Everyone jumped into the fray then, and the discussion raged back and forth for a quarter of an hour.

I was about to speak again when McEwan put a hand on my arm.

"Let me explain something to you folks," McEwan said firmly. "A police investigation does not take place in a vacuum. It can't be done back at the station with officers relying on memories and photographs. Finding a killer—or a thief—requires many hours of at-the-scene observation and questioning of everyone who might be involved—not just once, but many times. If you close the museum at this point, you will seriously impede our investigation. Granted, the immediate safety of your staff and collections is important, but your peace of mind and longevity as a museum depends on solving these cases."

"Do you have any extra men who could help provide security to the moving team and the museum staff, at least during the hours they are working?" the Dean asked.

McEwan laughed shortly. "Not from the Boston PD. But we already collaborate closely with your campus police department. There are two campus officers patrolling Wigglesworth Hall every day and night. It's not perfect, but it's more security than you had before Victor Fitzgerald's death." He turned toward me. "My suggestion is to let this very competent lady do her job and let us do ours."

A warm glow started in my chest. I couldn't believe that the same cop who'd been giving me such a hard time was now willing to support me in public.

The Board members looked at each other. "Dean Saltonstall?" Cabot said.

The Dean nodded at McEwan. "I want these crimes solved, and I agree with both Sergeant McEwan and Dr. Donahue. The museum will stay open."

Thirty

Same morning

Earlier that morning, James had realized that Lisa was stretched to the breaking point. After making a quick call to the hospital to make sure the CT scanning sessions were covered, he volunteered to stay home during the morning. Lisa had to be in early but he didn't have to be at work until two p.m.

Now James was cooking a late breakfast for Sam. Deftly, he flipped over the dollar-sized buttermilk pancakes that were his specialty and Sam's second favorite food—after spicy chicken tacos with guacamole. He pulled the real Vermont maple syrup out of the fridge; Sam hated the fake sugar syrup that Emma liked.

As he loaded up plates with pancakes, butter, syrup, and sizzling hot bacon straight out of the frying pan, he plotted how to get Sam to talk. Sam had passed his recent physical exam—performed by a regular pediatrician–with flying colors. As James had often told Lisa, going through medical school and a radiology residency hadn't made him good at diagnosing kids' ailments. And, as much as he hated to admit it, Lisa was right about Sam. The boy's difficulty wasn't physical; it was psychological. Lisa had tried—both to get James to pay more attention, and to make Sam discuss it—and failed. Now it was his turn.

James carried the loaded tray up the stairs to Sam's sunlight-filled bedroom. Sam sniffed the aroma of bacon like a little dog and lifted his head from the never-ending Monopoly game he was redesigning.

"Dad! That smells fantastic! Are you going to eat with me?" He surveyed the filled plates with something approaching his normal level of greed.

"You bet," said James, sliding a small table closer to the bed with one foot. He set the tray down, pulled up an elderly armchair—after removing a pile of painted lead Orcs, six goblins, and three dwarves—and eyed his son. Sam's eyes were bright and his color had improved.

"Regained your appetite, huh? Interesting. Barely an hour after Mom left the house."

"Uh—I'm never that hungry in the morning." Sam's gaze skittered away as he conveniently omitted to mention how well he'd eaten Sunday morning, when going to school wasn't an issue.

James took a big bite of pancake and chewed. Then he put his fork down and regarded his son steadily. "Sam, what's bothering you? We know you're not sick—the doctor said you were fine. But you keep missing school because of these vague tummy symptoms that come and go. Your mom and I are both worried, and your teacher doesn't have a clue what's going on. Can't you tell me about it?"

Sam emitted a gusty sigh and stared out the window. "Dad, you wouldn't understand..."

"Why wouldn't I? I was nine years old once, remember? I had problems at school, too. I was no good at sports, so I was picked last for every kickball game and every team event. I was thin and gawky and the girls made fun of me..."

Sam giggled and his hazel eyes fastened on his father's face.

James took heart and dredged up more details from his horrid fourth-grade past. "Some days, I scarcely made it home from the school bus stop without catastrophe. There was this huge dog, a St. Bernard, in the neighborhood that knocked me down at least twice. Then there was the neighborhood bully, Dicky Clegg, who picked on all the younger kids. I really hated him..." He paused as he noticed a sudden stillness in Sam.

"Are you being bullied at school? Picked on by one of the other kids?"

Sam hung his head and whispered, "Yeah. And I don't know how to stop him."

"Tell me about it."

It was like flipping a switch. Somehow, knowing his father had once been bullied was all Sam needed to talk. James listened with growing anger as the saga of Billy McFarlane emerged.

"Billy was teasing David Campbell at recess, poking him with a stick, really close to his eyes. I was afraid David would get blinded or something, so I went up and told him to stop it. We had a fight..."

Billy had not stopped there. He and his little gang of nine-year-old thugs had waited for Sam after school, dumped his backpack on the ground, and stolen his lunchbox. Then they teased Sam on the school bus, calling him a nerd and a wimp.

"Dad, I just can't think how to make him stop. I'm not very strong, and I'm not good at anything. I wish I could make Billy afraid of me, just a little."

It was a nasty problem. James had already established that Billy hadn't done anything bad enough to warrant calling in other adults. Most people would call it normal 'boys will be boys' behavior. What Sam needed was more confidence and some kind of physical skill.

Then he had an idea. He told Sam he'd be right back and ran downstairs to find the stack of Boston Globes that hadn't been recycled yet. Flipping through the issues, he finally found the ad that had caught his eye.

Back upstairs, James showed the page to Sam. "Look, Sam. Judo lessons. You could learn how to flip Billy onto his butt the next time he tries something."

"But Billy is huge—how could I do that?"

James smiled. "Martial arts teach you how to use an opponent's weight against him, so it works for small guys or for women confronting larger guys. It's all about balance and timing. I took a judo class once in college—I know you could do it. And look, this Level I class on Thursdays at six pm would fit our schedule. I'll take you. What do you say, Sam?"

Sam's face lit up with excitement. "You really think it would help?"

"Yep. You'll feel better, stronger, and Billy will learn to respect you."

"Okay, Dad! I'll do it. Can I start this week?"

James gave him a hug. "You bet. Now I'm going to call your mom and tell her the good news."

As he headed for the phone, he reflected that half of him wanted to share his news with Lisa immediately—the other half wanted to work off some of his guilt for not listening to her first. But semi-good intentions were not enough; when he called the museum, Lisa couldn't be found. Damn, now he was so eager to tell her about the breakthrough with Sam!

"Do you think she's in one of the third floor storerooms?" he asked the young student receptionist.

"Sorry. I'm new here, and I don't really know Dr. Donahue's schedule yet."

"Okay, then. Just leave her a message that her husband called with some good news, and say I'll try again later."

James replaced the phone in its charger thoughtfully. It was perfectly normal not to be able to locate Lisa in that labyrinthine building, but he was still uneasy. Was Lisa keeping the fact that there was still a murderer at large in mind, or was she hell-bent on solving the mystery and wandering around the museum by herself? His gut knew the answer to that one. Shaking his head, he climbed the stairs to change into work clothes.

Thirty-one

Thursday March 13, afternoon

"Hey, Lisa—there's another Celtic artifact missing." Ellen leaned on my desk so I was forced to look up from my computer.

"Oh, no. What is it this time?"

"An exquisite chalice from the Roault collection."

"The silver *repoussé* one?"

"Yup, that one. The most valuable one in the collection."

I rubbed my forehead. "It would be. Why is it that I work in a museum that seems to be the center of crime for the entire Boston area?"

"Well, if your job is the center of your universe—as it certainly is for you, Lisa—I can see why you feel that way."

Was that a bitchy comment? I decided to ignore it. "Okay, okay. Tell me how you discovered this one is missing."

Ellen pulled up a chair and plunked herself down. "Same way as last time. By checking inventory against a box I'd just opened."

"Any new clues about who might have done it?"

"Nope." Ellen tucked a lock of blond hair behind her ear.

I decided to live dangerously. "Do you think Dylan wants money badly enough to steal artifacts—"

"Don't start on Dylan again! Just because he dresses well and likes good wine doesn't mean he's a thief." Ellen paused, her blue eyes clouded with distress. "Oh, hell, why am I still defending him? He's a jerk. I should've known he'd be trouble when I found out he's the youngest son of a stockbroker."

"Youngest as in 'pampered'?"

"Spoiled rotten. He said his parents always gave him whatever he wanted." Ellen looked directly at me. "I finished moving out of his apartment last night."

I let out a long breath, not trying to hide my relief. No wonder she was a little bitchy. "Good for you. Where are you living now?"

"Sheila offered me her spare room until I find my own place." Sheila Howard was a friend of Ellen's from college who lived in Brookline.

"That's close to us. We'll have you over to dinner more often," I promised as I checked Ellen's face for incipient tears.

Ellen swallowed hard and then went back on the offensive. "Lisa, have you seriously considered anyone besides Dylan for the role of chief criminal?"

"Like who?"

"Tim Marsden, for starters. He's strapped for cash—owes thousands on his student loans—"

"How'd you find that out?" I realized I'd not asked enough questions about Tim.

"We were talking months ago about loans, and I said I'd almost paid mine off and Tim said 'Lucky you. I'll be ninety before I get out from under mine.'"

"Hmm. What else do you know about him?"

"Well, he's the only son of a research chemist and he lives with two M.I.T. students who are never there. He has a crush on Sara, who doesn't reciprocate his affections, and he gets upset sometimes..." Ellen stared at the wall above my head.

"So do we all. I know Tim resented Victor for slowing down his thesis progress. Is it more than that?"

"I think so. He took Victor apart after one of their meetings, said he was a stuffed prig who didn't know European art history..."

"That's not true!"

"...and he told me, only two weeks ago, that Valerie deserved to be boiled in oil for what she'd done to his latest thesis draft."

"So he joined the I-Hate-Val Club. I certainly felt that way."

"Yeah, but you manage anger differently. Tim carries his anger around like a cloud of bees," Ellen said. "He really doesn't give a damn about anyone else's troubles. Only his own."

"Hmm. Tim's a bit of a loner, I think. Dylan's gregarious and ah, very sure of his place in the world." I privately thought Dylan was a good deal more than self-confident; unscrupulous, sneaky, and totally narcissistic were some of the words that came to mind. He was a jerk, but was he a thief and a murderer as well? There was no proof...

Ellen's blond brows lowered briefly at my implied criticism of Dylan; then she remembered that she'd dumped him. "I seem to have a talent for picking selfish men," she admitted.

"You said it, but I thought it," I said. "Now, help me figure out a way to catch whoever's stealing our artifacts."

"Oh, so you're going to play Lone Ranger again? McEwan—not to mention James—won't be pleased."

~ * ~

After dropping Sam at after-school daycare, James plunged into his usual routine at work. He read CT scans, caught up on email, and met with the new X-ray technician to go over procedures.

When he ventured into the staff lounge to grab a late afternoon cup of coffee, he ran into Charlie Sloan.

"Hey, James! Did you hear our latest disaster?"

"No, what is it?"

"Someone's been playing hide and seek with a body from the morgue."

"*What?*"

Charlie slurped his own coffee. "Yup. It was in a body bag, on a gurney just outside the morgue. We were supposed to transfer it to the cooler, but we had a full house so it had to wait until we could shift one of the other corpses. When we came back to get the new stiff, the gurney had been moved clear down the hall to the elevator."

"Could it have been just a prank?"

"Maybe, but it's not the first time. Once I found a loaded gurney three rooms away, tucked into a storeroom that hardly anyone goes into except me."

James felt a twinge of unease. "Any idea who did it?"

"No," Charlie's face was grim. "But I mean to find out. I don't want to even think about what the newspapers will say if we lose a body inside our own hospital. I'm going to start with the *dieners*."

They tossed their paper cups into the trash and walked together towards the stairs.

"Where's your newest *diener*, Steven? Haven't seen him today," said James.

"Oh, he's over at the University. He has a second job, you know."

"He does? I thought he was full-time here."

"Nope. Works as a janitor-maintenance guy in some old building."

Alarm bells rang in James' head. What if the building was Wigglesworth Hall, the same building as Lisa's museum? Relentlessly, his brain connected the dots: a part-time *diener* who was way too interested in mummies, who also worked in a museum building that had a mummy collection, and who had access to bodies from the hospital morgue...

"Hey, James, what's wrong? You look like you've seen a ghost."

"I have to call the police. And Lisa. Tell you about it later."

James reached for his cell phone. It wasn't in its holster! He must have left it in his office on the charger. He abandoned Charlie and sprinted up the stairs.

Thirty-two

Same day, late afternoon

Ellen and I had hatched a plot to check out Tim's possible motives and recent activities. Ellen would go search Tim's office when she was sure he was busy in another part of the museum. In the meantime, I planned to look for evidence of stolen artifacts on the lower levels of Wigglesworth Hall.

A scene from an old movie niggled at my consciousness. Oh yes, Hitchcock's *The Birds*, when the heroine stupidly climbs alone to the attic while birds flap ominously in the background. I was dealing with human beings, not demented seagulls, but I had no intention of putting myself in danger. I checked my watch—only four pm. There was plenty of time for a quick reconnaissance before students and staff left the building. On the other hand, it was smart to keep in mind that Val had been murdered during business hours...

A stubborn little voice in my head told me that this was no time to act like a wuss. My two primary suspects, Dylan and Tim, were supposed to be working together this afternoon on the third floor; I'd check to make sure they were really there before descending into the dungeon.

I locked my office, ignoring the ringing phone—oh damn, I'd forgotten to check my messages—and hotfooted it for the elevator.

Inside the car, I reflected on Ellen's absolute refusal to think of Dylan as either thief or murderer and her interesting speculations about Tim Marsden. Granted, Tim had a better motive to murder Val, but I couldn't believe he'd really steal artifacts so closely related to his dissertation. My money was on Dylan for both crimes.

From the elevator, I had a choice of two routes to Registration because all the rooms formed a square around the core of Wigglesworth Hall. I took the right hand corridor and stopped just before the open door of our processing area. I heard voices.

"...get this load of boxes ready, then we can tape up the next lot. Man, am I sick of this job." That was Dylan.

"Yeah, well you always leave the heavy lifting to me, so I don't know what you're complaining about..." Tim sounded surlier than usual. Of course, the extra workload was taking him away from his thesis, so maybe his resentment was justified.

Thud. That must be a box being shifted. Then I heard the ripping sound of packing tape being torn off the dispenser.

Good, they both were safely occupied. I'd do a brief prowl of the lower levels of the museum building. If anyone asked questions, I was just doing my job as Director by making spot checks on the moving process.

The building's only elevator was now occupied, so I walked down the stairs in the southeast corner. The storage place for stolen artifacts had to be near a convenient loading dock, either close to the elevator on the first floor of this building, or in a tunnel below us that connected the basement to one of the neighboring buildings. I jingled my enormous key ring, now adorned with several master keys.

The door at the foot of the stairs opened next to a Coke machine near the main entrance. I turned right toward the elevator and ran smack into Tim Marsden.

"Tim! I thought you were working on the third floor today," I said as I rubbed my arm where it had bumped into Tim's surprisingly muscular chest. He'd gotten there awfully fast; he must have taken the other corridor and then ridden the elevator while I descended the stairs.

"Yeah, well Dylan just asked me to look for another dolly before we take boxes on the new route—"

"What new route? Aren't the boxes picked up and moved from the loading dock off this hallway?"

Tim mopped sweat off his face with the tail of his grubby gray shirt. "That's what we did until last week. Then Operations and Maintenance started a new project for LAS, so they took over the south driveway for all their vehicles and crap. They rerouted us through the basement, then the tunnel over to Noyes, then up to their first floor and out the north end of the building. O&M couldn't care less that it takes longer and makes more work for us this way."

I chalked up one more item Dylan hadn't bothered to tell me about and said, "You must have a holding area in the basement, then, while you're waiting for a truck."

"Yeah, we move the boxes in relays, depending on the number of dollies O&M leaves for us—the museum carts won't work for this kind of hauling. Naturally, we couldn't use any of the storerooms near the elevator—we had to make do with one around the corner, halfway down another corridor that's about half a mile away."

"Can I see it? I'm trying to get a better idea of the operation in case we can streamline it a little—make up for lost time. You know, with the murder investigation slowing everything down."

"Sure, I guess so. I have to go down there anyhow." Tim led the way back to the elevator and punched the button. The car swallowed us and descended with a jerk that made me recall the accident that had killed Victor...

As the car paused briefly between floors, Tim fixed a penetrating stare on my face and his voice sharpened. "You're not really checking on the moving operation, are you? You want to find the place where Dylan is hiding the stolen Celtic artifacts."

Tim's usual air of being put upon and helpless had completely vanished. Surprise made me stutter. "D-Dylan? Do you know for sure that it's Dylan stealing our stuff?"

"Yeah, that was obvious," Tim grabbed my wrist and practically hauled me out of the elevator. "I've been watching him for some time, trying to get proof. He's always sending me on errands—I figure that's when he hides the stuff. Stupid jerk—where does he get off stealing artifacts that I was planning to include in my thesis? He has to have another holding room, one no one else uses."

As his grip on my wrist tightened, hairs rose on the back of my neck. "Where are we going? And let go of my arm, please."

We passed through a utility room full of ductwork and roaring furnaces. Every bit of it looked ancient and ready to fall apart; I wouldn't be surprised to find asbestos insulation.

"Here." Tim produced his own key chain and fitted a key into a nondescript green door that swung open on well-oiled hinges. "I think this is Dylan's holding room, but I've never managed to be down here before without him." As soon as we were inside, he dropped my arm and flicked the light on.

I rubbed my sore wrist and glanced around, torn between a desire to get the hell out of there and my intense curiosity about the contents of the room. There were only a few boxes, lending strength to Tim's assumption that they'd been separated from the major loads being moved out of Wigglesworth Hall. As Tim lifted the flaps of the first box, which was not taped shut, I said, "Where does that door go?"

Tim looked up, his face flushed with frustration. "Another door? That's odd." He strode over to it and tried several keys until he found one that worked. The door opened into a small anteroom, with another storeroom just beyond.

The first thing I noticed was an odd smell... like wet leaves, or a clogged kitchen drainpipe.

Light spilled out of the inner room, and rustling sounds indicated that someone was in there. Holding my breath, I crept forward behind Tim.

I saw a table mounded high with a white powder. A human foot, its toenails painted a delicate pink, stuck out to one side.

Next to the table was a slight, brown-haired man holding two containers of Morton salt suspended above the body.

My first thought was that he was indeed an incompetent mummy maker since he was using modern table salt instead of Egyptian *natron*. He looked familiar; I thought it was the same guy I'd first seen pouring wine at the Greek vase exhibit reception. Was he also the man Sara and I had seen in the basement? I couldn't be sure—I had never seen his face up close.

Tim, his face beaded with sweat, advanced towards the top end of the body. He reached out and flicked away some of the salt heaped near the head, revealing long, dark hair, delicate features, and blue-tinted skin. Sara Browning.

Tim exploded. "What the hell d'ya think you're doing, Steve?"

Trying not to gag, I put a hand on his arm. "Tim, wait a minute. I know you were fond of her but—"

He flung off my hand. When he spoke again, it became appallingly clear to me that he didn't care that Sara was dead. "WHY DID YOU MOVE THE BODY?"

The man called Steve picked up a dissection knife. "Well, I needed a body." His voice managed to sound both reasonable and whiny. "My experiments, you see. I'm copying the ancient Egyptian methods of embalming. See, you have to take out the organs that putrefy—the intestines, liver, lungs, and stomach—and dry out the cavity with salt. Only I have the wrong kind of salt because I couldn't get over to Egypt—"

I swallowed hard as I realized that poor Sara's body had already been mutilated by this weirdo.

"Yeah, why *did* you move the body? Oh—and where did you get it in the first place?" The deep voice belonged to Dylan Luneau, who had suddenly appeared in the doorway.

My head moved back and forth, as if I were watching a tennis match. The real question was not who moved the body, but—

"You killed her, didn't you?" Dylan advanced into the room, his intent gaze fixed on Tim's face.

Tim's face flushed. "Fancy you asking that. You, the master criminal who's been stealing Celtic artifacts for at least six months!"

Dylan laughed at him. "I dare you to prove it! At least I'm no murderer! Which of you did it?" Dylan moved closer so he could observe both Tim and Steve.

Steve said, "I didn't kill anyone. I found this body just like I did the first one—"

Tim turned white and clenched his hands into fists. "Why you sonofabitch..."

"The *first* one! You mean Valerie Albrecht?" I cried.

"Is that the older lady or the young one? I like this one best because of her long brown hair. You guys sure made it easy for me, leaving dead bodies all over the museum..." Steve leaned protectively over his half-finished mummy and patted a salt-covered arm.

"Look out!" yelled Dylan as Tim leapt at Steve and snatched the long dissecting knife with its gleaming steel blade.

"You stupid janitor, you've screwed up my plans—" cried Tim, brandishing the knife.

I felt my wrist being grabbed—again.

This time it was Dylan, who pulled me out into the hall.

I resisted. "But he's got a knife! He's going after that Steve guy—"

"I don't mess with knives, and you shouldn't either! Let's get out of here."

I stumbled as Dylan towed me around the corner into a dim hallway I'd never seen before. I was scared and confused—it was hard to believe that my chief suspect was now my rescuer. "I thought you'd killed both women..."

"Oh, thank you very much. I told you, I'm not a killer." Dylan juggled his key ring with the hand that wasn't holding me and opened a door into another storeroom.

"But I saw you coming out of the Roman storeroom right after Val was killed!"

He said, "I found Val's body before you did. I was going for help."

"But—" My attention was diverted the bizarre contents of the room we were now in. It was filled with peas.

Yes, peas. Rows and rows of stacked, industrial-sized cans of peas... and corn... and green beans. "Food service storage?" I guessed.

"Yep. We're under Sanders Hall now—it's a Freshman dorm. Uh-oh." Dylan pulled the door shut as we both heard running footsteps coming nearer. "Sounds like Tim's looking for us. Let's stand on either side of the door and clobber him as he comes through."

Finding myself next to a tall stack of Green Giant peas, I picked up a can and hefted it.

Dylan flattened himself against the wall where the opening door would hide him.

I forced myself to breathe quietly so I could listen. The footsteps had slowed, and small clinking noises meant Tim was trying locked doors with his set of keys. If I survive this, I thought, I'm going to make sure far fewer people have access to master keys!

The door swung open and Tim stepped inside.

I bonked him on the head with the can of peas and he dropped to the floor. "Got him!" I crowed. "How about we—"

Dylan stepped over Tim's unconscious form and captured my wrists with one brawny hand. He used other to pull a handy roll of duct tape out of his front pocket.

"Hey!" I struggled futilely. "What the hell are you doing?"

"Putting you out of action, of course."

I screamed.

"Pipe down, or you'll get hurt. I don't know how much you know about my operation, Lisa, but I'm not hanging around while you tell McEwan what you suspect." He finished taping my crossed wrists together. Then he jerked me over to a convenient overhead pipe, raised my bound hands high, and taped them to the pipe. "You can turn in good 'ole Tim here for the two murders when the police find you, but I'm clearing out—with a few choice Celtic artifacts to fund my escape."

"But can't you tell me why—"

"Oh, do shut up! You're not my boss any more, so I don't have to listen to you."

I jerked backwards as Dylan leaned forward so his nose bumped mine.

"Nosy bitch. Too bad I don't have time to teach you a lesson." He reached up and squeezed one breast until I gasped. "Imagine suspecting me of murder—I'm really not that kind of guy."

I thought of several abusive retorts, but Dylan's proximity and my own helplessness made me decide not to scream again until he left the room.

Dylan pulled a rag out of his back pocket and stuffed it in my mouth.

Then he bent over Tim and neatly taped his wrists and his ankles.

"He won't be out for long," he said, chucking the roll of duct tape on the floor near my feet. Dylan walked to the door and flicked off the light. "I'm sure you'll have lots to talk about—if he decides to un-gag you. Bye, now."

~ * ~

James Barber's car careened around the last corner near the Museum's parking lot.

He'd called the museum, finally connecting with Ellen.

"Where's Lisa? It's important," he said.

"James, I don't really know where she is, but I suspect her of going down to the basement by herself."

"That idiot woman! Who does she think she is, Columbo?"

"Yep. I did tell her to wait until I could go too—"

"Two women against a murderer! Don't you know this is a job for the police? Jeez, Ellen, I know my wife is impulsive, but I thought *you* had more sense." James paused as he realized what he'd just said. " Sorry, Ellen— I didn't mean to take my worry out on you."

"You're upset—understandably. Call McEwan. Do you have his number?" She read it off.

"Thanks, Ellen." James punched in the number for the Boston Police Department.

"Sergeant McEwan, please. It's urgent..."

James pulled into a parking spot. He turned off the ignition and jumped out of the car. Across the lot, he spotted McEwan with a young colleague.

McEwan increased his pace. "Dr. Barber! I thought I told you to stay put."

"If it were your wife, would you stay put?"

McEwan smiled slightly. "Probably not. But a murder investigation is no place for amateurs..."

"I've got something that may be helpful to you. Lisa drew a rough layout of the basement when she was describing her first visit to the tunnels between buildings with Sara Browning." He pulled out a crumpled piece of lined yellow paper with "beer, milk, crackers, bananas, cheerios" on one side and a crude sketch of Wigglesworth Hall on the other.

"Huh." McEwan peered at it and then reached for his own map, provided by Operations and Maintenance.

The three men spread the two maps side by side on top of a handy Buick positioned under a streetlight.

"There," said James, pointing to a junction of a hallway and a food service tunnel on the O&M map. "That's where Lisa said she saw the man with the cart. I now think that was Steven Trendall, who I've just found out holds part-time positions in both the University maintenance department and my hospital's morgue. Steven has an unusual interest in Egyptian mummies."

"You mean he kills people so he can make them into mummies?"

"I don't know if he's murderer—he may just be a body snatcher. My colleague in Pathology told me someone tried to steal a body at the hospital."

McEwan frowned. "I don't like the way this is all coming together. Okay, you can come, Barber, but you'll fall back when I tell you to. Got it?" He patted his holster as he moved rapidly towards the entrance to Wigglesworth Hall.

The young officer, who hadn't said a word, followed.

James brought up the rear. Perhaps it was just as well he'd never taken up target practice and never purchased a gun.

Thirty-three

Same day, evening

The darkness settled over me like a musty winter coat.

It was quiet down here in the basement. Too quiet, especially since I was tied up in a room with a murderer. How far away was Tim, six feet? Close enough that when he came to and discovered he was not alone he could harm me—if he freed himself before I did...

The gag tasted horrible. It took me nearly five minutes to spit it out. Then I tried to loosen the duct tape around my wrists. The sticky stuff was now twisted into a rope, but I couldn't feel where the ends of the tape joined because my fingers weren't long enough and my hands were taped over my head. But the tape had ripped most of the hairs off the skin of my wrists, and the loop was fractionally looser than it had been.

Disjointed thoughts ran through my head as I struggled to slide one hand against the other and out of the loop.

...Too bad I'm not wearing a ring with a sharp-edged gem.

...I wish I could sit down, my legs feel like they're coming unhinged at the hips.

...Wonder how long I can wait before I pee in my pants?

A rustle and a groan from the floor made me freeze. Tim Marsden was waking up.

"Shit. Fuck. Who the hell did this to me?"

I heard him writhing around on the floor, moving closer to my feet. I stepped back as far as my bound hands would let me.

Tim rolled across my shoe and slammed into my legs.

"Arrgh!" I yelled.

"Lisa, is that you? How the hell did you end up in here with me?" Then he grunted. "My head hurts."

I figured there was no point in silence. Maybe I could keep Tim busy until someone came. "I conked you on the head with a can of peas and Dylan tied both of us up with duct tape."

"*Peas?*"

"Yeah. We're in a food service storeroom with a shit-load of canned vegetables." I took a deep breath. "Just out of curiosity, did you kill that guy Steven?"

"I've no idea. I left him bleeding in his horrible embalming studio."

"But you did kill Val, didn't you?"

Tim let out a long sigh. "That bitch was planning to have my thesis—not just the manuscript, but the whole topic—thrown out by the committee. She said it was 'substandard scholarship on an indifferent subject,' as if she actually knew anything about Medieval Art. It was bad enough that she kept pissing all over my drafts. I couldn't let her get away with it. I'll never get an academic job unless I get the PhD..."

"You'll never get any job at all, now that people know you're a murderer."

"Depends on whether I actually go to jail, doesn't it? Ha! That's one hand free..."

Tim's newly released hand brushed my leg and I jumped. I hated having him touching me, but I forced myself to stay put so I could keep track of what he was doing. *If only I could see...*

"I think I have a Swiss army knife in one of my pockets... yup... now if I can get the damn thing open..."

Tim's body vibrated against my left knee as he sawed away at the tape. Did he have both hands free now? I had to keep him talking. "Why did you kill Sara? I thought you were in love with her."

"I thought she was pretty, yes. Sara saw me moving Val's body. I was coming out of the elevator with the corpse on a cart. I hadn't covered her properly—a foot was sticking out, and Sara spotted it. So I snuffed Sara and put her into a disused storeroom. But while I was doing that, someone snitched the cart: that little creep Steven."

So that's why you looked so odd when we discovered that Val's body had disappeared!

I heard the tearing sound of duct tape parting. Frantically, I yanked my hands down as hard as I could.

It was no good. Both hands remained firmly taped over my head.

There was a massive slithering over near the door and then the overhead light flicked on.

When my eyes adjusted, I saw an unbound Tim standing in the middle of the room, about ten feet away from me. His eyes showed no expression at all as he regarded me.

"You know too much, Lisa."

My pulse accelerated. "Tim, killing me won't do you any good. Dylan will turn you in."

"Dylan is only interested in saving his own skin. He'll have left town by now. Which is why you have to go." He took at step towards me, Swiss Army knife held ready in his right hand.

I screamed.

The door to the storeroom swung inwards with a crash. "Drop that knife!" said McEwan. His handgun steadied at the level of Tim's chest.

The knife clattered to the floor.

I sagged in my duct tape handcuffs. The room spun around me and went dark.

~ * ~

"Wha... what?" I muttered as someone cut the tape around my wrists.

"Shhhh," James said, catching me as my arms fell to my sides and my knees buckled again. "You fainted, but you're going to be fine."

"Ow," I said as he began to rub my arms to bring back the circulation. My head felt very strange, as if it were semi-detached or stuffed with cotton.

"Damn fool woman..."

That was my husband again, but I could tell he wasn't mad—just relieved.

"Why the hell did you have to go into the basement alone?"

The walls stopped moving and James' face came into focus. "I wasn't alone, I was with Tim Marsden—"

"Who's a murderer twice over!" His expressive eyes shot off green sparks.

Now he was pissed.

"Yeah, but at the time I thought the murderer was Dylan—"

"For someone who deals with facts, you have a remarkable tendency to jump to conclusions!"

"But..."

McEwan interrupted us as he strode into the basement storeroom. "Save the recriminations for later, you two. We've got Marsden in custody. Now, are you okay, Ms. Donahue?"

"Yes. My arms feel like they're on fire, but I'm fine. Where's Dylan Luneau?"

"We're looking for him. Look, we need to go down to the station and get everyone's statements. I can promise some hot coffee."

I turned to James. "What about Emma and Sam?"

James pulled out his cell phone. "I'll ask Tami from next door to pick them up and feed them hotdogs or something."

As we reached the elevator, the doors opened. I wasn't surprised to see Ellen, dressed for the outdoors. She gave me the once over and then said to McEwan, "The museum's closed up and everyone else has gone home. I'm going with you. I want to know what happened to Dylan—"

"We need information from you in any case, Ms. Perkins. You can ride with Richards."

~ * ~

The Boston PD had a meeting room that resembled our staff lounge in terms of battered furniture. The only difference was that all their chairs matched—and they were all equally hard.

I slumped in my seat and sipped at the blackest, bitterest coffee I'd ever tasted until James appeared at my elbow with three sugars and two creamers. I doctored my coffee and inhaled the hot, sweet liquid. Now that I was sitting down, my body ached from head to toe.

"How long have we been here?" I asked James. McEwan was arranging a lawyer for Tim Marsden, who didn't have one of his own.

"Only about twenty minutes," he said with a sympathetic smile. "Your sense of time is probably screwed up."

"You could say that. I feel like a week has passed since this morning." I glanced at my wrist, but my watch had fallen off sometime during the scuffles in the Wigglesworth basement. Instead, I had a band of reddened skin where the tape had chafed.

I turned to Ellen, who was rummaging around in her black leather purse, the kind with thin straps that could turn it into a backpack when needed. "What happened to Steven?"

"The body-snatcher and mummy-maker? He got hauled off in an ambulance, but one of the techs said he'd be fine. Lost a lot of blood, though." She held up half a chocolate bar—Ghirardelli, the semi-sweet variety. "Hey, look, sustenance!"

"Ellen, you're a lifesaver," I said.

"I know," she said smugly.

She broke it into three pieces, and we munched away.

James rose and prowled around the room. He always paced when he was upset or nervous—I figured he was both right now.

Ellen said, "Lisa, did you notice if Dylan—" She stopped when McEwan walked into the room.

"Okay, folks. Marsden now has a much better lawyer than he deserves, and Luneau's legal eagle is on his way—"

Ellen interrupted him. "So Dylan's in custody?"

"Yep. Caught him exiting one of the tunnels under Noyes Hall. As I was saying, when the lawyers show up, I sure have a lot of questions that need answering. In the meantime, I need to hear exactly what happened in that basement, in the order it happened." His grizzled eyebrows lowered in my direction. "You start, Ms. Donahue."

I told my story, aware of gasps—Ellen—and rumbles—James—from my audience. I left out the part where Dylan grabbed my breast, figuring that little detail was hardly relevant. "I think Dylan's motive was money—"

"That fits," said Ellen bitterly. "He was always buying expensive gadgets for the kitchen. And you should see his wine cellar!"

I glanced at her with sympathy. Poor Ellen, she must be feeling awful, not to mention duped.

"I'm horribly disappointed, but on the other hand, it *is* a relief to know Dylan's not a murderer," Ellen said, reading my mind.

"So you did have questions about him, after all," I said.

"Yes, I did," she admitted. "But I was doing my best to bury my head in the sand."

James patted Ellen's shoulder. "What about Tim's motive? Was it really just Valerie getting on his case about his thesis?"

I shuddered, remembering Tim's transformation from nerdy graduate student to knife-wielding maniac. "He hated Val, that's for sure," I said. "But it was more than that. He was hugely frustrated in at least two areas of his life. Ellen told me about how he was in debt. Also, he was the sort of scholar who can never finish a really big project. Perhaps because then he'd have to leave the safe, familiar life of being a perennial student and actually get an academic job."

Ellen summed up. "So, Tim's motive was revenge, Dylan's was money, and Steven was—is—just a kook." She looked at McEwan. "Did any of them have anything to do with the computer virus that screwed up our database right after Victor's death?"

McEwan shook his head. "No, that was George Skirvin, getting back at the museum for firing him."

"The place is full of kooks!" James said. "I'm beginning to think being weird is a requirement for anyone going into the museum business."

"Yup," Ellen and I said together.

McEwan slapped his notebook on the table. "This is the damnedest case," he said. "Instead of just one criminal, we had three—four if you count the cyber crime.

I think I'll tell my chief that if anything else happens in this building, he should assign it to someone else!"

His voice was rough, but I thought I detected the ghost of a grin on his face. McEwan would come back, all right, if we had another murder in the museum.

What was I thinking? If we had another murder, I'd be on the hot seat since I was the Director!

From the somber way James was looking at me, I could tell he was thinking the same thing.

A young policewoman stuck her head in the conference room and spoke to McEwan. "Sir, the lawyers are here."

"Okay, ladies and gents, you can go home now. I don't want to see your sorry faces for at least twenty-four hours," said McEwan.

~ * ~

We drove Ellen home to her friend Sheila's apartment. I turned around to say goodbye before she climbed out of the back seat. "Will you be okay, Ellen?"

She gave me her trademark grin. "Yeah. Maybe not right away, but soon. I don't like admitting you were right, Lisa, but my intuition knew Dylan was bad for me. In fact—" she included James in her glance—"I've made a vow not to start dating again until I meet someone really special, someone who has long-term potential."

"Your biological clock is ticking?" James said.

Ellen snorted. "Perhaps. Or maybe that's it's just that I'm tired of wasting time. You guys go together like salt and pepper—it sets a good example for the rest of us." She hopped out of the car and waved.

"Not a bad exit line," I said, as James changed into second gear.

He laughed. "Ellen will find what she's looking for; I'm sure of it."

"I hope so." I rolled down the window to let the fresh, rain-scented air into the car. Ellen's love affairs reminded me of my younger self, trying on relationships like different costumes. Experimenting with new looks and lifestyles to see which ones fit. Just what Emma and Sam would be doing as soon as they became teenagers.

"How's Sam?" I asked as James turned onto Massachusetts Ave.

"Oh! I haven't had a chance to tell you—problem solved." He sent me an apologetic smile. "You were right. The problem *is* at school, and it's a bully."

"Who?"

Quickly he filled me in and told me about the upcoming self-defense classes.

"That's brilliant. You're brilliant. Thank goodness." I sagged in my seat. "Hey, why are you stopping here?"

James parked in front of our favorite Italian restaurant, Guido's. "I know you don't want to cook, and the kids are taken care of, so how about a little *tortellini all panna con funghi* and some wine?" He waggled his eyebrows suggestively.

"Oh, what a good idea!" I said, suddenly finding the energy to let myself out of the car and cross the pavement.

Soon we were seated at a cozy corner table with candles and a red-and-white checked tablecloth. The waiter, whose name was Angelo, recommended an Italian red wine and brought hot, fresh bread with some garlic-basil oil for dipping.

A few sips of wine and the heavenly aromas from the kitchen behind us revived me miraculously.

James waited until we'd ordered before he dropped his little bomb. "Actually, there's something I wanted to discuss with you without the kids around."

"Oh?" I sensed something big was coming, but had no idea what.

James took a deep breath. "I've been offered a five-month fellowship at the University of Illinois Medical School in Urbana."

"James! Good grief, when did this happen?" I actually put my wine glass down.

"Well, you know I've been longing to get out of the hospital environment and do a stint of research." He explained how he'd been searching the Internet in odd moments at work for an "ivory tower" position. This fellowship would allow him to write a couple of articles on tropical diseases and delve into some other interests he'd shelved when he took his first job after medical school. "It would be from September to December, only five months—four and a half, actually, since I'd be done a week before Christmas. I know the kids wouldn't want to leave their schools, so they'd stay here with you. But my stipend would be enough that we could afford to travel back and forth on weekends."

Hmm. On the one hand, I'd be a single mom again during the week—with two kids instead of just one. On the other hand, this might be the perfect opportunity to cement my relationship with Sam. And my lawyer father would always be able to suggest a third point of view.

"It could work, but we wouldn't be traveling all that much. I'd be stuck here some weekends for museum functions," I said slowly.

James tipped more wine into my glass. "Your Directorship is going to be very demanding—I'd do most of the traveling to see you and the kids."

"That would take some of the heat off me."

We went back and forth, discussing all the pros and cons.

He was certainly right about the job, but how could it be more stressful than this past semester? Besides, it would only be for a few months. I remembered all the times James had supported me. I looked at him, saw the gleam in his green eyes, the eager way he leaned toward me. I smiled.

"Can we do it?" he asked.

"Okay, but I have a condition," I said, retrieving my wine and taking a large sip.

"What?"

"Remember how we were going to take a trip to Italy? How about this summer, before our commuting marriage starts?"

His grin was positively smug. "I've already asked my mother if she'd take the kids for two weeks."

"You planned all this!"

"Yup." James motioned to the waiter and ordered champagne.

Soon the frothy elixir filled our glasses. I raised mine high. "To Italy—"

"—and Illinois. Cheers," he said.

Meet

Sarah Wisseman

Sarah Wisseman writes the Lisa Donahue archaeological mysteries. She hadn't a clue that she wanted to be an archaeologist until she traveled to Israel right after her freshman year in college. There she ate falafel, fell in love with Jerusalem, camped illegally on Masada, and spent a month at the excavation of biblical Beersheba. Once hooked by archaeology, she returned for her junior year at Tel Aviv University, an experience that eventually inspired *The Dead Sea Codex*.

In her day job, Sarah is an archaeological scientist at the University of Illinois. Her research project on Egyptian mummies led to the Lisa Donahue mystery, *Bound for Eternity*. Her fourth book, *The House of the Sphinx*, is set in Egypt.

*VISIT OUR WEBSITE
FOR THE FULL INVENTORY
OF QUALITY BOOKS*:

http://www.wings-press.com

*Quality trade paperbacks and downloads
in multiple formats,
in genres ranging from light romantic
comedy to general fiction and horror.
Wings has something
for every reader's taste.
Visit the website, then bookmark it.
We add new titles each month!*